Unzipped
Sixteen

Hallie Hart

PRAISE FOR *UNZIPPED SIXTEEN*

"Hallie Hart is the next E.L. James with this riveting novel of innocence and seduction!"

Caroline McBride, novelist

"The Unzipped series by Hallie Hart is an absolute must-read for any discerning female. Juicy, seductive, and completely compelling, you can't put them down. Hart shows insight into her incredible international life through her modeling career, and the lusty males barking at her door. Learning through her alcoholic and drug-addled mother and her life growing up in Manhattan, and on the French Riviera. Prepare to learn a few things!"

Lucia Gillot, Staff Writer SPIN, European Editor WONDERLUST, New York Metropolitan Magazine, Yahoo, AOL

"Brimming with lush detail. A true conversation starter, one that you will have you debating with yourself long after you turned the last page... is this fiction or not?
Celebrities, fashion, sex, drugs, money, love, hate... all the makings of a steamy novel!"

Steven Lyon. Film maker and Editor in Chief, The Indulge Magazine

First published in Great Britain by House of Hart Publishing in 2023

Copyright © Hallie Hart 2023

Design by Softwood Self-Publishing

ISBN: 979-8-9884589-0-6 (paperback)

ISBN: 979-8-9884589-1-3 (hardback)

This work of fiction, including its characters, events, and plot, is the product of the author's imagination. While certain characters in this novel may bear resemblance to real people, their identities have been changed and altered significantly to ensure their fictional nature and protect the privacy of any individuals who may have inspired them. Any resemblance to actual persons, living or dead, is purely coincidental.

CHAPTER I

Allie is.. or is she?

How should I title my story? Fuck. No, not fuck, that was just a pitiful sigh. Ooh, I've got it... "One too many brilliant days in the life of a sexy woman-child that made herself a muse," and so it is written. No, that's not it either, since my story is one-half fiction and one-haf nonfiction, I should call it: "The truths and untruths of an innocent girl who learned to forget in order to survive her scandalous life and famous so-called friends." Yes, you heard me right, my shameful little secrets could be buried in a book of fiction *oh so* easily. After all, who could dispute it? Curious now? Stick around, my *unzipped* narrative starts here.

I grew up a part of my life in small town bum-fuck-nowhere Pennsylvania, and the other half in wicked cool New York City. I lied about the Pennsylvania part to strangers, it's not a Gucci kind of place; it was more like a country inn, knitted quilts, horse farm kind of place. A nothing place that left me with a faded and lousy memory. I prefer to just erase it. What can I say?

I'd been lying to myself for so long, approximately twenty years. How did I do it? I felt I had no choice; I know everyone says that, including the bad guys in movies, but to imagine a life outside of this ugly place I was born, I had to lie to escape it. I was never there. I might as well have been a ghost floating above my life; the reality for me was that I didn't exist.

I was born for greatness (in my head), and swore I would get it, bleed for it, do anything to move from this life. I just didn't know how. I used to pray, no, not pray, swear I would escape this shell of existence I felt like I was living. I was always, I know it sounds like a cliché, different than everyone else. Not, in my opinion, the most beautiful girl, but was nearly at the top of the most unusual girls, or as some would say, odd. So many fantasies of grandiose plans... I was going to be a princess, a famous actress, and a singer. Everyone would love me. Well, some of that turned out, but not too soon. There is much to tell before I let you in on all the fucked up, glorious shit I've been up to in my devilish existence.

By the time you finish this read, you will have been highly emotional because of my life; intrigued, turned on, or completely disgusted and saddened. I hope you fall into all these emotions throughout my story. I'm feeling all kinds of things, just remembering some of this shit as I pound away on my keyboard. I mean, I have to dig deep into the depths of sin, pain, passion, and hysteria. It's not serial killer binge-worthy like True Crime, but it's some fucked up shit. Bukowski-worthy, in my opinion. I'm here to talk about the glory of my days becoming a viper and the hell of being born to one. One thing I hope that takes place from the pages is that I get the therapy everyone thinks I desperately need. Hah, laughable treatment; I would probably lie to the therapist, so it wouldn't really work, would it?

I learned at an early age that being mischievous regarding sex appeal was in my favor, and my dear ol' mom taught me all about it. Yes, lovely, bipolar, beautiful mom taught me how to use my womanly powers for good or bad or...both? My mother Tory would walk into a room with her long, strawberry blonde hair, piercing green eyes, rockin b cups, and long legs. She would light it up like nobody's business. She dressed like a fashion model, or at least I thought so. There was nothing like her in this one-horse town, well, except for future me. "Mom," that's funny. I wasn't allowed to call her mom; she made me call her Tory and pretended to be my big sister. I went along with it. I'd almost rather she be my sister since she didn't have a maternal bone in her body. That woman was a real dream-nightmare for all the boys. They saw exactly what they got, and they loved being in her web. She was the ultimate man stealer, man manipulator, equally innocent and naive.

I think half of her was good, but I never did get to see much of that version. She was also wildly unpredictable, sometimes disappearing for days when she was off her crazy pills. I referred to them as "her crazy round thingies." Who knew where she went when she left me? I could never dig the truth out of her, she felt it wasn't any of my goddamn business, so I stopped asking. To tell you the truth, I would pay anything now to know where that woman actually went. I often dreamt of her coming back as a loving version of Tory. A mother that would cook eggs or yummy pancakes in the morning when I came downstairs, but yeah, you know, never happened. I was the cook, the mom for little me, and actually loved to cook, go figure.

To this day, Tory is driving her fourth husband insane. I'm shocked he isn't on some sort of medication himself. To add insult to injury, Tory was also a violent drunk before she began her fixation on cocaine in my early teenage years. Damn, did she love her coke! I didn't realize what was what initially, but I got educated very quickly. My mother made her money from trading stocks and real estate. Later in life, she explained that coke helped her "stay in the game with the boys." I didn't know who this woman was when she was high, but wow, did she throw some amazing parties! Especially a couple in particular. One was my eleventh birthday party. She had a live ten-piece band, a dance floor, of course two bars, swinging couples, and a pony for the kids. I'm still not sure this party was for me, but all one hundred guests and the band sang Happy Birthday to me. At that time, I felt special, like Pippi Longstocking had found her mother, or at least for one day of her life.

All of that was short-lived because a raging Tory got into a car accident late that night after I went to bed, around one a.m. It was serious, we couldn't find her for 48 hours. She had gone off a cliff in the backwoods of our beautifully overgrown property, jamming her Mercedes into the trees, suspending the car ten meters in the air. Tory fell out of the dangling car and laid in the forest to die. I forgot to mention that it was in the fall, and the Autumn weather is cold at night. We got her back, we all thanked God, but I don't think he had anything to do with it. Just like a cat she had nine lives. Tory had hit her head pretty badly and couldn't speak for a week, she was pretty messed up, but then by the "grace of something," she snapped out of it and was back to her feline self like nothing ever happened. I remember seeing her wake up and thinking that she had never looked more beautiful... why did I think that? I'm not entirely sure, but this goddess woke up smiling, and for me, that smile was all I needed at the time. Tory grabbed my hand, squeezed it, and slowly lipped I love you. Short-lived, the first night out of the hospital, she went to a local bar to get some attention from some random men and get her fix of coke and ego.

Listen, I loved her, and she somewhere in her sick mind loved me too. Tory couldn't get right with anything. The demons would fight for the drugs and alcohol; she was as much a victim as I. Although I loved seeing her high sometimes, she was so childlike and funny to play games with. One time she surprised me after school with a golf course she had made for me. The funny thing is, it was indoors.... yes, in the house. We started the first hole upstairs on our third floor. (We had a big ass house, yes, we had a bit of money; if we didn't, I would not have ever got out of this small town). Tory occasionally surprised me like it was the best day of my life. Making the golf course, playing with me, knocking out windows and breaking lamps was her way of saying fuck it, we can do whatever we want without consequences. Her way of not growing up, her way of saying fuck you to her mom who didn't understand fun or love her for that matter...

Tory's mother, my grandmother, grew up in hard times. Her parents came to America with two children, and by the time they were done, they had ten. My grandmother, Eve, was born in the USA in New York City but didn't have her parents for long. They both passed by the time she was eight. Eve never told me what happened to them, and I never asked. Eve and her siblings were raised by themselves; instead of giving up, they worked. As soon as she was old enough, my grandmother worked as a girl serving booze in a seedy lounge in Lower Manhattan. I am sure the fiery redhead had to endure a lot for a thirteen-year-old girl. She became naturally hardened and cold from her life.

A strict and complicated woman that was not very nurturing to my mother growing up, nor in her adult life for that matter. Eve did well in the restaurant industry, enough to provide a good education to my mother, but made sure she was sent to the best schools far away from home.

At the tender age of fifteen, Eve met and married a man seventeen years her senior and began having all of her five children: Tory, Katherine, Sherry, Julie, and Jeffrey. My mother however didn't start out with the name Tory, she changed it from Nancy, a name she despised, when she'd decided to reinvent herself after college. My grandfather was a grumpy, yet quiet man, worked extremely hard and made his fortune in real estate. Yes, my grandmother married someone of great means, and she learned how to spend it immediately. She was also a beautiful woman and smart, so she typically wore the pants in the family. Guess the apple doesn't fall far from the tree, does it? She and her husband William moved out of the Big Apple and into a suburban, middle-class area in Pennsylvania, which I still hate to this day. That is where I was born… but since my mother was sent away to a nice school outside of this place, she had a real taste for the opulent, and with that came the idea of moving me out as soon as she could. Tory worked between New York City and her home office in Pennsylvania until she hit some big numbers on Wall Street.

She met my father, a sly Italian businessman (that's how she referred to him anyhow), living in Manhattan when she was right at the beginning of college, and had me. I never got to know him, other than his occasional checks on my birthday. I don't think he cared too much, but she despised him more than anyone. I still can't figure out what the fuck he ever did to her or anyone for that matter. Tory just had a way of just hating people and discarding them like they were the lowest thing on earth. I know he must have helped her financially because she would have demanded it, and also, I saw her bank statement that had large deposits monthly.

When Tory had the money she thought she needed, she moved us to the Upper East Side of Manhattan in a beautiful penthouse. She paid for it all upfront. Tory used to say that she never wanted to owe anyone, and she didn't. She just took from everyone.

But shortly after we began to play our golf game, she pushed me down and said, "clean this shit up and do it now." She pushed me quite hard. There was so much blood on my arm from where I hit the corner of the glass table, I may have needed stitches. Most likely, I did; I have a scar as a reminder. Tory occasionally would push me away from her like a dog. The fact I was a skinny kid was not beneficial. Let's see, scars…? One on the back of my head was a bloody gash from hitting the fireplace. I'm thankful for this one, on the line of my eyebrow, because it doesn't show. Five on my arms, ten from the waist to my toes, and the one on my top lip later became a signature mark for me as a model… thanks mom, I guess. What's ironic is that she doesn't remember, and I don't remind her. I pretend like nothing ever happened. Actually I don't pretend, I just don't feel that it did; as if I was watching it as an observer. Isn't that strange? So fucking strange.

CHAPTER 2

Lost and Found

I remember another "fun" birthday, at least at the time, I thought it was. I think about it now, and I'm confident it was left in that little girl's heart; I now see it as an inglorious memory. One of many twisted tales I have embedded deep in my heart, until now, feeling hurt as I half-smile. Tory needed to get out of New York for some reason. She was pretty anxious that summer day in July. The reason I remember is because I was turning sixteen. Also, I met a police officer at the airport in Paris, yes police and in Paris, handsome like a fairytale prince....how and why will follow. For me, the only great escape was wearing my rose colored glasses. It was not necessarily a defense mechanism; it was more like a lonely kid making up stories in her head to feel important to the one person who didn't really see her.

Tory took us on an incredible first-class plane ride, where she'd often disappear to the bathroom and drink one Champagne after the next. She asked me if I wanted a glass; I, of course, wanted to be just like her and said yes in my delirium. Bonding time was upon me. Moments after my first divine taste of the pink fizzy drink, the young flight attendant, shocked, asked Tory to stop giving alcoholic beverages to a minor. Tory agreed, but as the woman turned, she told me, "down it before she comes back." Of course, I giggled with her and did what she suggested.

Interestingly enough, I remember my first sip like it was yesterday. Bubbles were divine and sweet, yet bitter. I really flipped over the flavor; I called it the "grown-up soda." My friends tried to make me drink several times, but I never wanted to until now. I think back now; I would have done anything she asked just so I could get some kind of approval from her.

When we landed in Paris, I had to pee badly. I ran into a bathroom, yelling to Tory that I would hurry and be right back. Tory never waited. She was too high and too excited to get to where she was going. When I returned moments later, she was nowhere to be found. Tory had a driver waiting, never turning back to find me, or even remembering I was with her. Some witnesses said the woman I claimed to be my mother met a man and was kissing him in a car. Apparently, a lover was on the forefront of her brain, not an innocent kid like me.

I was found emotionally distraught running around the terminal. A sweet, older French lady brought me to an officer that spoke English to me. I remember my 'knightly' officer, blue eyes and black hair, tall and very slender. He had a softness about him that immediately calmed my weary sobs. I told him my mother's name and that she had a disease of the brain. Therefore, she may have lost me. I think he understood what was what. He looked unconcerned to me, but I am sure he was anything but. I asked him not to leave me until my mother came back, oh now I remember his name, Gerard. Gerard stayed with me for what seemed like an eternity, but the paper he wrote on in front of me said 'Trois', which is a French word I know. It means three.

I pretended not to understand French, but unfortunately for me, I did. Three long hours of small French cakes, to this day, I still love Madeleines. Daydreaming while I sat with him, making up stories of Gerard and me, meeting again in the airport, plunging into one another's arms, vowing never to be apart. It was all interrupted by my mother Tory running into the room yelling, "Where the hell did you go, Allie?" Stumbling over my words, she dismissed me. I think everyone around me thought that I was just a kid that wandered off, except for my prince Gerard. He looked at me with great sadness in his eyes, sadness like he wanted to save me from my life. He didn't though.

CHAPTER 3

The Kindness of a Stranger

When we left the airport, we met her "friend" Dominique. He greeted me kindly with a flower. I think back now, he must have pulled it from the planter near the car, but nevertheless, he was kind and considerate. I liked him right away; he was one of the good ones. What I mean by "one of the good ones" is that many of Tory's boyfriends weren't so nice. He took us to the beautiful Four Seasons Hotel in Paris, near the Champs-Elysees. "Wow," I couldn't keep my lips closed. I was literally drooling on myself; I must have been so hysterical to look at. Dominique spoke perfect English, and I got an opportunity to speak French with a real Frenchman. I was taught French for three years in school, so I felt I was doing pretty well. I was in the most breathtaking place in the world. I didn't think anything bad could happen to me in such a remarkable place. I'm sure something could've. Well, something did occur to me, but it was more... enlightening. I guess some would say it's disturbing, but nothing really gets to me the way it does to most. I think this may be a family trait.

Dominique was a tall 6'2", blonde haired, blue eyed, incredibly movie star-worthy, attractive man... Memories of him are embedded for my lifetime. My mother and Dominique immediately went to the bar after the bellman took our bags, where they ordered Champagne. Dominique handed me a tiny version of theirs, yes again, "grown-up soda." I was dizzy with happiness, and the bubbles had me beyond tipsy. After a couple of glasses of pink delight, we headed to our suite.

I had never seen a place this big that was a hotel room. It was called the Eiffel Tower Suite; I mean, I look back on this and think, "this man was loaded." I was wowed, again and again, exploring the suite's enormous rooms, each room filled with the loveliest long, purple flowers in humongous vases. I could not imagine a more opulent place. As I pounced into the living room, the bellman entered, another man with a silver tray with a flower. My mother and Dominique were kissing as they entered the vast room, but Dominique quickly noticed the man with the tray and greeted him.

After tipping, Dominique softly leaned over me and said, "le plateau est pour toi petite princess." I giggled because I knew what he said, and I was more than thankful. My smile of all white teeth was proof enough for him. Dominique popped me up on a chair at the dining room table while my mother was off pouring a drink. He opened the round, silver top off the tray, and there it was to my delight.... my very first French dessert in France; crème brulee! It was so rich and creamy, yet a sugary burnt top made it so divine. I ate it slowly; I remember wanting to make it last a lifetime. I stopped doing that after that day because I could have it so readily now. Laughing, he went off looking for Tory. I guess it was his time to get something a little sweet.

CHAPTER 4

Embrasse Moi

I walked around the boundless rooms with curiosity, every bit of it was stunning, bold yet subtle. I recall the contrast of colors and fabrics, lush and feminine... just simply rich. I knew then I was in the right place. This would be in my near future if I had anything to do with it.

I heard my mother making odd noises, but I knew what they were doing. I had seen it with my own eyes at eleven years old. I also knew how it all worked, sex, that is. After my first, accidental "porn view" of her and a lover, Tory sat me down and explained everything in a not-so-nice way...her way; direct and crude... just like a cowboy, not John Wayne, the other assholes. After that, I'm sure she took a Xanax and passed out. That was her M.O. for day drinking and day fucking.

Dominique came to pass the time with a Johnnie Walker Blue Label scotch. I remember it because he explained it to me as he sat on the sofa in the living room next to me. Chatting about architecture, fashion, the notorious Louvre Museum, growing up in glamorous Paris. He went on and on; I was so engaged. Everything he said was magical, falling from his French accent like music in an orchestra. My eyes wandered around his chiseled face. Dominique's sandy blonde hair fell perfectly, full, and shiny, and his eyes, oh his eyes... they smiled when he spoke, and his lips, so kissable, so full. I loved looking at him, he was beautiful, but he was comforting and warm. He spoke to me like I was someone. I wondered what it would be like to be with such a man; handsome, intelligent, sexy, rich… very rich.

Then it happened, to my surprise, he asked me…"Have you ever been kissed?"

I shyly smiled and said "no," replying boldly, "but I have thought about my first kiss."

"You have? Tell me, what did you imagine?" Asking sweetly, Dominique seemed to be genuinely interested. I felt like I had a new friend and was more comfortable around him than most.

"I would be kissed passionately. I would just know it was the right man for my first," explaining like a naïve girl. I couldn't believe the words falling from my lips. This was such an inappropriate conversation, this person was with my mother, but I couldn't help but stare at him with puppy dog eyes.

"That sounds really nice. Do you know what a French kiss is?" Amused, he waited for my answer.

I softly responded, "yes, kind of." Like a curious, trustworthy girl, I then asked, "Is it with tongues?" I waited for his answer. I think he was contemplating his next move or words.

"Would you… would you like me to show you? I can do that, but we must keep it a secret between the two of us…but I want to show you, Allie." Lowering his voice as not to be heard. I, of course, loved the idea of keeping secrets from my mother, so my smile became a grin.

"Yes… I would like that very much," responding slowly to his offer. Dominique stood, lifting me into his arms; my feet

18

barely touched the ground. He wrapped my arms around his neck. I felt as if we were the only ones on the planet; I could hardly breathe. He pushed his mouth on mine. I was slightly uncomfortable as he began exploring with his tongue. It felt strange, but I let him continue without an ounce of resistance and began to actually enjoy it. As he kissed me profoundly, pushing further into my full lips and mouth, I responded, I felt experienced, and it felt good. We kissed for what seemed like forever, but only ten minutes had passed. Pulling away slightly, he took my hair out of my ponytail and began kissing my neck softly. He said he loved my deep, green eyes but, "they would be even more beautiful if my dark hair were to frame them like a piece of art." I loved what he was saying and doing to me. I had forgotten all about Tory and was only seeing him.

I think back to this day. Wow, I was a child and so inexperienced. I could have trusted a bad man, but I didn't; I trusted one of the better ones. Dominique was going to take me on a journey of self-discovery, and I was ready for it. At least a part of me thought so at the time. Pulling slightly away, he sat down from our kiss, placing me onto his lap. He was rock hard as he began to rub my pussy softly through my summer linen pants. I was nervous. I never had a boy, let alone a man touching me, but I didn't want it to stop. It felt too good; I was wet from his strokes. I understood what was happening because I had been touching myself for years. Rubbing me slightly harder while working my clit. He knew how good it felt because I moaned softly with my eyes closed. Dominique slipped his hand down my pants; I was ready.

I still couldn't believe it was happening. He rubbed my wet privates like he had done it a thousand times. He knew my body and I couldn't hold on any longer. I was on the edge of ecstasy, and there it was, the most divine, hot sensation rushing through my body. I came in his skilled hand; it felt so good. I didn't know if I was ashamed or thrilled; I didn't know anything. Dominique gently pushed me aside and went to the bathroom, where he cried out in pleasure from what I thought was the same release I had moments before. I don't have ill feelings for him. I didn't want it to stop. Part of me was so immature; the other wanted to explore more. He would continue to kiss me the same way every day when Tory was knocked out cold for a week and a half. He never pulled my clothes off or removed his. One week with my Dominique; I felt lucky to have him. He was keeping me safe because of my kisses. We were bonding. I knew he wouldn't let Tory do anything terrible to me. He called me angel, and for the very first time, I felt like one.

When I thought about my first time, I always dreamt it would be someone that looked like Dominique. Someone tall, foreign, built, full lips, well dressed with some foreign accent, the kind of man that would make women wet when he walked in a room. Kind of like the hot soccer players or Ralph Lauren model playing polo, yes like that. He would be well dressed and versed, making everyone laugh their fake laughs at parties. He would only be looking at me, while every woman in the room drooled all over themselves while shooting me daggers at the same time. It makes me laugh now, but that is exactly what I got, the man everyone desired. I actually look back now and feel I manifested the entire thing. I still do it to this day.

After the third day, Dominique took me shopping. It was a high-end boutique, very sexy, called Christian Louboutin. He had me try on all the heels and told the ladies I was his friends' daughter. The ladies flirted with Dominique, and were super attentive to our needs, offering us Champagne. They poured an entire bottle while we were there. He bought me my first heels, kitten heels. "Louboutin! Louboutin!" I chanted in my head. Later in life, I would walk in dozens of pairs. He lit a fire of desire, a painful need for power, and the possession of material things. Well, that's not all true. Tory might have had something to do with my wardrobe.

CHAPTER 5

Alone at Last

Dominique was a highly educated man. He shared all sorts of knowledge, from school to the importance of getting what I want out of this great big world, law, and the art of reading people. The art of reading people would later become one of my "superpowers." He planted the need-seed to make money and find my great escape from my mother. Around my sixth day in, Tory wanted to go to London. She pleaded with Dominique to take her. He diplomatically said he was sorry; work would be pressing in the following days. He offered to send her alone and have someone watch over me here at the hotel. Wow! She leaped with joy before rushing off to pack a small bag. He gave her an envelope from the safe, I could see it was a bank envelope, she smiled and kissed him on the cheek goodbye. I went to hug her, but she said, "Please, do you want mommy to walk around in wrinkled clothes?" And walked out. Ugh, I thought, "Mommy? Since when!?" I was happy she was leaving, beyond happy, because I could finally be alone with Dominique.

The door slammed, and she was gone, just like that, once again like all the other times. This time was different. I wasn't alone for the first time. Turning to me, Dominique smiled. I ran immediately into his arms; he was hard as he began kissing me. Only moments later he had carried me to one of the bedrooms. I really thought I knew what I wanted, but did I? I'm so unskilled... I was confused. My mind swirled with all kinds of things. I wasn't prepared for all the grown-up stuff, but something inside me screamed, "yes!" Gently he placed me on the bed, kissing me tenderly, "Allie, can I take your shirt off?" He pleaded, needing to see me. "Yes." I nervously whispered. Slowing down while watching my reaction, almost like he was studying me; he began to unbutton my shirt. With each button, he got closer. He lifted me to slide my arms out of my blouse before laying me back down, softly kissing my perfectly shaped breasts, pulling at my nipples gently with his mouth while gently moving his hand into my pants. He pulled my underwear to the side, moving his fingers slowly against my lips, making my flower wet. "Ah, I think I love that!" I cried out.

"I know you do; I feel it dripping, my little angel. Are you going to cum for me?" Asking me to cum, made me want to even more even though I didn't know my body quite yet.

"Yes, yes, my love! I want to!" He played with me a little faster, yet very gently teasing my privates. I came hard! This time it lasted longer and was much more pleasurable. Pulling his pants down, he exposed himself, "please, Allie, can you lick me?" Begging with his hard cock in his hand.

I did. I wanted to please him; I had this enormous crush on this older, experienced man. I licked it as he told me to, not taking it into my mouth too far, just on the head to make him squirm. I did as he instructed for a while until he moved me softly back and asked me to kiss him, pulling me up to his mouth. Kissing me deeply, driving his tongue in my mouth repeatedly, I could feel his hunger grow. He needed more of me; he couldn't contain it any longer. Was this it? Was he going to have me? I was scared, yet the idea of pleasing him made me happy. Dominique laid me on my back and pulled my pants off. His cock was so hard, his eyes so intense, you could see how much he desired me.

I didn't know what to do or how far to go with him. My nervous energy was in tow, but my heart was leaning towards him now and I had fallen for him. There wasn't really a choice now, was there?

I trusted him, so I listened for the next words of direction. Dominique laid on me but didn't penetrate me. He groaned and grinded against me... It felt good; I was getting more excited. I was ready to be a woman. I wanted him to make love to me.

"Please take off your panties angel. I want you to climb onto my face. I will show you what to do." Explaining carefully, I followed his lead. I could see the hunger and delight in his beautiful blue eyes. I sat gently on him as he began to work the shaft of his manhood with vigorous strokes. I naturally started grinding on his face; he loved it. He brought out a little beast in me, and I longed for the unknown. Eating away like a hungry animal, he couldn't get enough. It was like he had never had something so good in all his life. This turned me on. I moaned and moved to the rhythm of his mouth until I could not hold on, I felt the hot liquid come out of me, "Oh, oh, oh," I whimpered as I came on his face.

Dominique couldn't hold on either anymore. He leapt forward with me in his arms, slightly startling me, and laid me on my stomach. My face was turned to the right, but I could see him. Dominique was stroking his long, hard manhood and now was at the top of his threshold. Screaming out the loudest, most pleasurable sound while cumming on my ass. He laid on my back, planting small kisses on my face over and over gently, then whispered, "Allie, I love you." I loved him too but was afraid to say it out loud. Dominique moved off me, pulled me in, and cradled me in his arms. I thought about what would happen next. My head was all over the place. I was afraid of being alone again, but my thoughts were interrupted.

"Why don't you go get a shower, angel" Pulling me up slowly.

"Ok." Moving as he suggested. I felt like I was walking on a cloud.

Peeking into the bathroom, he asked me if I would like to go on a dinner date with him. I smiled from ear to ear in my hot shower and squealed out, "yes, yes, yes!" Amused, he informed me something was waiting on the bed. I dried off quickly and ran to the adjoining room. It was a huge silver box and a small gold one. I opened them; the larger box was a beautiful deep blue dress. I think he called it ultramarine, I know he did because later it would fall off my lips as an artist as 'klein blue'. The dress was quite lacy. I had never had anything so, "adult-like." It was a sleeveless dress with lovely, delicate silver buttons. The dress was shorter than I was accustomed to wearing, but I was thrilled to see it was a few inches above my knee. I opened the other box, a small silk heather gray handbag, and another pair of heels. This time, the heels were higher, and I was stirring inside with excitement. I felt like he was my boyfriend and I, his girlfriend. Gushing inside, I went to the bathroom and put on some of my mother's makeup. I knew how to do it because I watched her do it daily. I didn't put too much on, just enough, and Dominique felt it was the perfect amount to bring out my natural beauty. I looked years older. I could only imagine what was in store. Dominique greeted me with a glass of Dom Perignon, and we toasted. "You look beautiful, angel. You're gorgeous!" He conceded. I felt pretty because he made me feel so.

CHAPTER 6

Our First Date

Dominique asked me nicely to not touch him or kiss him while in public. He told me that it had to be our secret. I agreed; after all, he was much older. People might think it was strange, which could be weird for me. That's what I thought the most bizarre part of all of it was? Can you believe the tiny mind of a blossoming girl wanting someone to love her?

The night was utter bliss; everyone knew him and said their "hellos" to me. I wasn't invisible to him or his friends. For the first time, I felt adored and special; It felt right. The restaurant was on the smaller side, very dark, with small red votives placed all over. The place was primarily styled in structured, black rounded banquets, with red flowers lining the contemporary glass tables. It was a den of indulgence, and it was like no other place I had ever been. At Dominique's request, I tried the tasting menu. I had never had so much delicious food, full of fascinating flavors in every bite. Almost as fascinating as the beautiful people surrounding us. I would later find out that getting a reservation there was simply impossible. We finished our decadent meal and wine. "I say we get out of this place." Leaning into me, now more relaxed about his affections.

We headed towards the exit, where the head chef/owner approached us. He kissed Dominique on both of his cheeks, "so French" I thought, then kissed my hand as he called me a "belle fleur." The chef/owner of one of the highest-end restaurants in Paris is kissing my little hand, wow, it could not have been any more amazing. We said our goodbyes, exited and got into a car with our driver heading back to our hotel. On the ride back, Dominique told me stories of the people we met at the restaurant, making me laugh at the things he shared about them. Intimate things about their lives and how they felt more important than they were. I knew who else in my life felt that way, my mother, Tory.

When we arrived at the room, he excused himself to make a call. He asked me to please contact Tory and see how her trip was. Then just as soon as he left, he walked back into the room and said, "You know what, I will call her, not to worry."

"Ok," I responded quickly. I can't lie. That, to me, was a great relief. I ran off to my bathroom to wash my hands and look at myself. I started to study my face. I wondered why I didn't like what I saw for so many years. I looked and felt pretty, my long full black hair, my green eyes with a hint of brown in one, my full lips; even fuller bottom one, long limbs and nice breasts, cute ass... I really liked myself for the first time. Smiling in the mirror, I was beaming with happiness, but I needed to write it down. I ran to my room, grabbing my journal for a few moments, not wanting to forget to outline my evening. I could fill in the blanks later. Isn't that what a good writer is supposed to do? Or so I've read in Cosmo or something like that. I wrote quickly. I didn't want him to see; it was very personal.

CHAPTER 7

My Silk Number

I returned to the living room where Dominique was, just as he said goodbye to my mother. He told me that she would be there longer and not back for another three days.

"Can you stay with me a little longer? Till she gets back?" I asked while holding my breath.

"I can't imagine wanting anything more right now, Allie." Confessing to me his strong desire to stay, made me believe in him. He was the first real adult I had trusted.

Dominique suggested a bath in the enormous Victorian claw tub in the bathroom. I, still a little shy, said yes but was looking down. He came to me and lifted my chin up. I will never forget the look he gave me, so loving and sincere.

"Angel, you are beautiful. You should never think otherwise." Pushing my long hair back. He told me I was magnificent with his French accent. "Magnificent?!" I couldn't contain myself; I was bursting inside. While filling the bath, he came to me. I was nervous as he unbuttoned the front of my dress, slipping my panties to the ground, picking my feet up to remove them. My thoughts were swirling again, but I took his directions with ease. Next, removing my bra, he began kissing the front of my breasts. He brought me closer to him, picking me up to press my naked body against his fully clothed one, kissing me passionately as I began to melt. He then undressed, signaling for me to get in with him. He had brought Champagne to the bath with us, popping it while he continued to nibble on me ever so softly. We drank the entire bottle; the room was getting hot, and so were we. His tongue was so warm and inviting, in and out of my full lips. We had chemistry. For me, it was a first, not knowing myself as a woman, yet I wanted more. He would make sure I had it.

He pulled me from the water, took me into the bedroom, where there was a small gift bag laying on the bed. He presented it to me proudly, "that is for you, my angel," waiting patiently for me to open it. I was jumping up and down. I could not believe another gift; how did I get to deserve this?!

"Thank you, thank you!" Giggling, I was overwhelmed by his generosity. Grinning a little at my innocence.

"Anything for you, but...I think it's time for you to know something." Pausing carefully as not to alarm me.

I got a little less bouncy to adjust to his more serious tone. "What is it?" I stared at him with a concerned look.

"No love, no long face. I just wanted to tell you that I care for you. I haven't spent so much time with a girl in a long while. I don't want it to end. Allie, I will be here for you through anything you may need. That is all I wanted to say to you. You're my little angel." I ran into his arms, hugging him. I began to sob. He said to save the tears for unhappy times. He stated that this was not one of them as he began to kiss me. I felt him all around me for the next minute, holding me tight, caressing me.

Opening the box was fun, something I would get used to later in life, but I couldn't wait for now. Inside was a long silk lingerie number, with an extensive slit up the side and a lovely backless plunge. I was not sure why I was so happy, but it might have been the fact that I was getting gifts and love, yet I was nervous, not sure what I was going to do in three days. I could never go back to the way things were, or could I? He asked me to put it on in the other room and come back to him while he would wait in our bed. I did as he instructed. At this point, I would have done anything he wanted; I trusted and loved him to pieces already. I went to my mirror in my bathroom, put the silk number on, and went back to the room where he laid in our bed with just his pants on. I stood in front of him so that he could look at me before inviting me into his bed. I loved this man! I wanted to give him my virginity. I felt like a woman waiting to be born. Touching me as I stood next to the bed, then directing me to lay on him, I did, and we kissed. Putting his hands around my butt cheeks, pushing me into his hard manhood, grinding on me. It felt so good; I loved it. He knew what to do to me; I was flooded with emotions.

I trusted him, so I would take his lead, and lead he did. Laying me down, he slid up my lingerie, exposing my wetness. Playing furiously, but gently with my honeypot until I couldn't take it any longer, and I let out the hot liquid. He loved what he could do to my body. I could just see it in his devilish smile. "That's my girl, my love, my sweet little angel." Dominique would say. These were words I would often hear in my future. Putting his mouth on my special spot between my legs. Licking it lightly, spreading me like a flower. Teasing me until my privates were pulsating, my body was shaking, I could not take anymore.

I was so wet again, and again, oh, it felt so good. I didn't want my orgasm to stop... I loved it; I loved him with every fiber in my body. Pulling his large, pulsating penis from his pants, he asked me sweetly in my ear if he could enter me. I pleaded, "please be gentle, please, you're my first."

"I will, my angel, I will. I promise I will never hurt you. I'm going to go slow." Putting his mouth on me, he became more aroused as he kissed me passionately. Pushing his manhood against my clit, rubbing it all over, it felt good. I was getting aroused again, my hips started to move naturally.

"I'm going to put it in now. It'll be ok, I promise, my sweet angel." Slowly my love entered me. It was painful, but I let him stay there without saying a word. I wanted my virginity gone, to know what it would be like to enjoy it.

"Are you ok, angel?... Oh, Allie, oh Allie," Pushing harder now, he kept going.

"Don't stop," I whispered. I was in pain, but I wanted to please this man I loved. He was deflowering me. Why else would he want to be with me otherwise? He only stayed inside me for a short time and then lost his mind; my tightness drove him insane.

"Oh... oh...oh angel, I am going to explode now!" Crying out at the top of his lungs, the man was losing his mind over it. Pulling out, he finished with two strokes on his shaft, finishing it off all over my stomach. He quickly grabbed a towel and cleaned me up while I lay in bed, then cuddled me like a protector. Feeling loved by this forty-year-old man was everything. I was just sixteen, but now a woman, or at least I thought I was. I felt safe for the very first time. I don't think everyone had the same blissful experience that I had. I remember clearly how I felt; intoxicated by him.

CHAPTER 8

Surprise my Angel

He woke me with a kiss and my first Mimosa the next morning. Telling me we had a big day; we were going on an adventure. I stood up and asked, "Where are we going?" with a giant goofy smile.

"Come here first," Tugging gently at the ends of my long hair, pulling me into his arms and back in bed. Kissing and touching me, he told me we were going to a famous museum called the Louvre. I knew the museum and its reputation, but he told me that the curator owed him a favor, that we would go with him on a guided tour, not all of it, but what he loved - Modern Art. I was always interested in art, and little did I know that Dominique would be the man who influenced my decisions regarding it later in my career.

We playfully rolled around in our bed, touching and kissing. It wasn't long before he wanted me again. Dominique wet his fingers, putting them on my pussy, making it ready for his entry. Crawling on me slowly, grabbing his hard cock, he pushed into me slowly. I welcomed him for the second time as I put my hands on his back. He leaned further into me, "I love you, angel." I was startled by his words again.

I smiled at him and said, "I love you so much." Just the way a girl would say it, so sweet and innocent. It was the first time it came out the way I wanted it to.

I am not sure if this was wrong, but it felt so right at the time.

I was mad crazy for this man. I felt like a woman with him, although I am unsure what he looked at me like. I'm not sure at all. My mother was his age, and apparently, he liked her as well, but I didn't dwell on it because I was in love. Finally, someone looked at me, really looked at me, and heard my voice.

This time, I was more at ease; I rocked my hips with his. I relaxed as he made love to me. I waited for his moves and tried to follow them. Kissing me deeply, over and over, he pushed. I know now that he was holding on for dear life. He could barely breathe he wanted to cum so fucking badly. Begging me to never leave him, he let go, "Allie, I have to have you. I'm cumming, angel." He had for as long as he wanted me; I was his.

Dressing soon after our quick showers. Dominique poured us another Mimosa, and plated some fruit and croissants. I loved French life; I didn't want this to end ever. I started to cry in my drink. I don't know where the emotion came from, years of hell with Tory, lack of being noticed, fear of losing him, my life in general? Dominique came to me quickly, asked me what was wrong. I told him I didn't want to leave him. How can I keep him? Smiling, he asks me not to cry, that he would find a way to see me. He swore he would. My tears stopped, but I excused myself to wash my face. I returned ten minutes later calm and collected. I hadn't let my walls down for anyone ever; it was relieving. Dominique may have done naughty things to a young lady, but what he also did is make me feel free, in some sort of way.

Dominique decided the museum could wait till tomorrow. He made two calls, one to the curator and the second to the desk, to bring his car around. He would be driving today. "Are you up for an adventure?" Asking with a devilish grin.

I jumped into his arms and said, "yes!" Entertained by my pure nature and enthusiasm. "Where are we going?" Asking as we walked.

"Just wait, angel." He replied. We went outside, and I was impressed yet once again.. There was a silver and midnight blue Bugatti Chiron. I know about the Chiron because every boy I knew drooled over it. He was cool, I mean, his cool factor was already up there, but now it's completely bonkers and beyond. Opening my door, "my lady." I jumped in, overjoyed, and impressed to the nines. He was really alive, flesh and bone in front of me, stealing my innocence and my heart.

How? Why? ... I kept repeating this to myself, and then it happened the tears were back. There was no stopping them. We were driving by this time. Dominique realized what was happening and swiftly maneuvered the car off to a small street. Jumping out of it, he ran to my side. "Princess, why the tears? Do you not want to go away? I'll do whatever you want me to do. Please tell me." Pleading with me.

"I just don't know why you would want me......why, no one wants me?" Sobbing now at this point, I tried to catch my breath.

"You are so precious, an angel sent from heaven, Allie. I'm so lucky to have met you. I know you are so young, but I feel connected to you. You make me so fucking happy, that is why.

36

You are so fucking beautiful, smart, cute, and funny to be around...you are the whole world in one breath. I love you!" He tenderly held my face in his strong hands. I listened to his words and slowly stopped crying. Feeling reassured that he cared for me, I knew he wouldn't let me go. I found a smile through my wet cheeks. Dominique lightly wiped my face with his shirt and kissed my wet pouty lips.

"I love you, Dominique. I really do," kissing him back.

"Everything will be just fine; I won't let you go, Allie." Assuring me as he pulled me into him. He knew what I needed to hear and just how vulnerable I was. Part of me still felt like I could shatter at any second. I think he knew that too. He might have liked how fragile I was. A tiny porcelain doll, so delicate and beautiful.

We drove to the Le Bourget Airport, where his private plane was waiting. All of the staff seemed to know him at the terminal. I felt like royalty; everyone was super, sticky-sweet to me. Walking through like we owned the place and straight onto his G5 jet, I knew this plane, but who didn't? I glimpsed over at him, and then in front of everyone, he put his arm around me. Walking me to the steps of the plane, everyone saw this. Wow, I was shocked and thrilled, too much to ever describe, elated beyond words. He acknowledged us. This was a first, but not a last.

Hitting the first step, I asked, "Dominique, what shall I wear? I didn't bring any clothes." I could hear him behind me as I walked onto the plane.

"Well, my angel, I think I know your sizes by now, don't you?" I looked down the aircraft lane, and to my delight, the entire back was filled with designer gift bags. "I know you had a birthday a week ago. I took the liberty of having some nice things picked up for you to wear." Squeezing my ass, then sat down to watch me squeal a bit. I think my reaction alone made his day. "I also had my assistant make some appointments for you at a lovely salon that has a spa. You, my birthday girl, shall be pampered before dinner." I turned and thanked him, "where should I start?" I wanted him to tell me so that I would please in whatever way I could.

"Princess, sit down. I'll have Cindi grab them for you to open." Signaling to the flight attendant. Dominique instructed her to bring the bags after takeoff and to pour the bottle he selected.

The rosé Champagne was crisp, cold, and delicious. "Happy Birthday, angel." Dominique held his glass up to mine.

"Thank you, my love." Tapping his glass. There must have been twenty bags. Designer heaven. I had Louboutin's, Alexander McQueen, Chanel, Gucci, Prada, Dior, Balmain, Tom Ford, and lastly, a Harry Winston box. I was so happy; I didn't know what to do with myself. Is this man really in love with me? He must be the one. I mean, this shit doesn't really happen. Or does it? I opened all the boxes in the order he suggested. The beautiful clothes and bags were something straight out of the covers of fashion magazines. This felt like a movie... You know, the older man and the younger woman, or younger something. He leaned in and softly pressed his lips on my hand before laying a box within them. "I saved the best for last." Opening the box in front of me like a prince in a Disney film. Honestly, you can't write this shit; it was so fucking perfect. And even more perfect was what was inside...It was a bright green emerald. Ironically enough, it was an emerald cut. It was big, and I mean huge. It took the entire area between the knuckle and my hand. I was so mesmerized by it. I would later find out that this beauty was five carats and flawless. I know now that this carries a hefty number.

Jumping into his lap, showing him my hand, I kissed him all over his gorgeous face. "Thank you, I love it, I absolutely love it!"

"It's my greatest pleasure angel, I needed to find the perfect ring to match your eyes...well, except for the slither of brown."

Explaining my eye color in detail. He noticed my tiny spot of brown. Wow, I was floored. I don't even think Tory ever said anything about it in my entire life. Dominique was building his doll and grooming it too; me. I didn't know at the time, but he made little Allie his everything from the ground up. I was adorable. With the right clothes and makeup, I was sure to pass for "of age," or at least people wouldn't be talking about us. That is precisely what happened.

CHAPTER 9

St. Tropez

We landed at 10 am, he took me straight to the posh spa and salon. Dominique kissed me and lightly shoved me off, "go have a good time, and I'll be back at two to pick you up."

"Yes sir, good time, sir," laughing, I saluted him and entered the salon. The receptionist was in tow, waiting with herbal tea and a smile. I really needed a little alone time, so this was perfect. I had a massage, body scrub, three-course lunch with Champagne, hair, makeup, and lastly, a course in "how to keep it all just so." I was so beautiful to even myself now. My heart was fluttering; it really was. I had butterflies in my stomach, so much that I was jumping out of my skin to see him. Actually, more so for him to see me. Pulling up precisely at two o'clock, he turned up as promised, but this time in an Aston Martin DB9. He looked more 'James Bond' to me in this car.

I didn't tell him, but I had brought a change of clothes and a pair of heels from the plane. I wanted to finally have an opportunity to surprise him. I wore a soft plunging v-neck, dark green, cashmere Akris sweater. I paired it with an off-white, skinny, low-waisted pant and a beautiful sling-back silver Chanel pump. Dressing the way I did, you would have thought I was twenty-one, which I thought would please him, and it did. My long, thick, black hair was parted to the side and styled by what the salon referred to as "beach waves". I had never heard of this hairstyle, but I knew one thing, it made me look sexy. I was clueless about my hair, but that would soon change. Dominique enthusiastically jumped out of the shiny silver car. He also cleaned up, changing into a beautiful navy-blue blazer with a polished light gray collared shirt. He wore dark jeans, gorgeous brown lizard-skin shoes, and a Hermes belt. Wow, that man was beautiful; I felt like the luckiest girl in the world. He would forever change me and the mere existence I was living. This was just the beginning of our adventures, I didn't think it could get any better, but for me, it did. This didn't last forever and ever but long enough for me to think about it for years and years to come. He made me a woman; I still owe him the gratitude of thanks.

My prince and his chariot, this can't be real. Look at us, a real couple.

"Wow, angel, you look beautiful, absolutely stunning, you literally take my breath away. You are so fucking divine."

Spinning me around, he was eager to look at all of me. For now, I was the happiest young girl pretending to be a woman in the world. I couldn't help but kiss him, but I pulled back quickly. I was unsure how I was supposed to act with him because he requested that I not touch him in public. I know now that he needed to upgrade me to a young, pretty woman, not a girl. He didn't hesitate this time. Pulling me in, he held me for what felt like an eternity. "You are mine." I smiled and said yes. We drove for a while and got to an exclusive, residential beach street, where he owned a house. His home was architecturally modern, enormous, and perfectly polished, precisely what I expected from my love. My thoughts went to Tory for a minute, only that I couldn't understand why he would want to be with her, but I

41

forced myself to erase the bad thoughts from my head.

Dominique came around the car and opened the door. Romantically picking me up, he took me inside, walking through slowly, placing me on my feet.

"Let's have a drink. Would you like that?" Asking sweetly.

"I would love some bubbly if that is alright," I replied hesitantly.

"Yes, look at me, anything for you, my angel... anything." Reassuring me to not ask but to answer. I think back now on these times. He must have been having the best time. I was a young, impressionable girl that would do anything for him. I'm guessing that made him want me and want to take care of me. He either convinced himself I was twenty-one, or maybe the harsh truth is that he got off on knowing I was sixteen and could dress me to look older to satisfy his urge to be naughty with me. I would say maybe a little of both. It kind of turns me on to this day, I have to admit.

I found myself floating after my second glass of Champagne, asking if we could lay down for a bit. I followed him to the master suite in his vast and contemporary home. His house was mainly white with large, modern paintings; Pollock, de Kooning, and Motherwell were famous artists he had collected. I felt like I could live inside of those paintings. They were mysterious and evoked a desire to know more. I expressed my feelings on the art, he suggested getting painting supplies and giving it a try. I thought to myself, why not? Anything seemed possible, right?

Entering his bedroom through two large black doors, there was an entire living room and a fireplace in this space. The bed had a velvet tufted, navy blue headboard that went all the way to the ceiling. It had luminous silk, light blue sheets to match. It was chic and elegant. Dominique played some soft lounge music in the background; the scene was set for sex.

"I need you. Is that ok for you?" Touching my ass lightly. It felt good; I wanted more. "Yes, I want you to need me."

Caressing his arms and back, his frame was magnificent. I was spellbound; my happiness was almost impossible to contain. He asked me if he could take off my clothes. I, of course, said yes. Gently removing everything of mine, folding it while placing it on the bench at the foot of the bed. He stayed dressed for a bit longer, kissing my mouth deeply, quickly turning to my breasts, then between my legs to my no longer virgin privates. His touch was soft, lightly licking me, bringing my hips closer into his mouth. I cried out as he went faster in circles on my sweet spot. My head was dizzy. I felt like the room was spinning from the pure joy I was feeling. Moaning deeper, he knew so well he had me. I came after what seemed like an eternity of teasing, I came so hard, but this time he didn't stop. Dominique would not let up, he continued to lick and pull my swollen clit with his mouth, and again I released over and over. This was my first multiple orgasms. Wow! It was sublime. I was shaking from the intensity; I absolutely loved it and him more so than minutes before. He knew how to look after me. He wanted this, or at least at the time, he believed so, as did I.

Directing me to unbuckle his pants, begging to be touched with my mouth. I could not deny this man anything. I really did not know what to do; I wasn't skilled at oral sex. I only ever kissed his penis. I told him to teach me, he did in great detail. I complied; I only wanted one thing to please my new boyfriend.

I took his manhood in my hand, into my mouth as he guided me to give him head, the same type of pleasure that he gave me. I sucked, licked, stroking his cock until I could taste a little of his juice. Pulling me back after ten minutes, removing me from his throbbing cock.

"You're too good at that angel. I had to stop you. I don't want cum yet; I need to make love to you." Whispering while placing me on my back. Entering me slowly, my pussy dripping wet as he slid inside. Inching slowly in, as to savor every moment of me.

"I love you, Dominique!" Professing my love. Pushing faster, he stayed deep inside of me.

"Allie, oh Allie, I love you too, angel." Letting out a cry as he filled me up with his semen. He collapsed, "I'm sorry, Allie, I couldn't stop myself. I didn't know that was possible."

Apologetic for his mistake. "What is it you're sorry about?" Whispering in his ear.

"I came inside of you, my love," mumbling the words in embarrassment. I shook my head at him, presenting a slight grin.

"Not to worry, I'm on birth control, a birthday gift from you know who." Reassuring him that my mother put me on the pill, not because I was sexually active. She just didn't want to take any chances. He kissed my forehead; I could see his sigh of relief. I don't think either one of us wanted a baby. I couldn't even take care of myself yet.

"I meant what I said, Allie. I love you." Cradling me in his arms. The bond between us was growing. I felt it. I was utterly, madly in love with this man.

"I know you do." Closing my eyes, I was content.

I must have fallen asleep in his arms because I was startled when I woke. I didn't know where I was. Smiling, the images came washing over me like the most exhilarating feeling I'd ever imagined. I was in awe of my life. I found a floor-length pink silk robe next to me. I put it on, walked through the long, beautiful halls filled with striking images in black and white. The photographs were by the famous photographer Annie Leibovitz. I was again drawn to the art. The prints were edgy, some nudes; these images, in particular, intrigued me. The freedom, being naked, felt good as I was just getting to understand my body, and of course, the older man helped me to realize it much quicker than most.

I entered the kitchen, where an older woman was prepping for dinner. She instructed me that Mr. Dominique was waiting for me in the study at the other end of the house. Walking through the enormous rooms and halls, feeling like a princess in her castle. I tapped on the open door, he smiled.

"Come please, you don't need to knock," waving me in. That made me feel important. My mother and everyone else in my life never wanted to speak to me, knocking, well this was a must in my home. My grandmother disliked everyone, my mother, just my father and me... well, he died when I was twelve, but my father did love me. He tried to see me often, but Tory wouldn't let him. She was also "The Punisher," the punisher of the "only man" I loved as a child. I would not allow her to take the second man I love; Dominique. I needed him; he was a lifeline for me. I got scared for a second as I thought about it, could this happen, could he be taken from me? My ill-feeling quickly went away when I saw my beautiful man perched before me.

Dominique signaled, tapping his leg for me to sit on. He rubbed my back generously, asking if I were happy. I, of course, told him how elated I was, that I couldn't describe it if I tried, but soon my happiness would turn to dread.

"I just got off the phone with Tory." Blurting it off without thinking, he crushed me. I didn't want to hear her name today. What did she want? Am I going to have to leave? All of these racing thoughts rushed over me. I was fearful of the following words that would come from his beautiful lips.

"Hey, I can read you so well; your face gives you away, angel. There is nothing to fear. I handled it, ok. I expedited her funds, so she could enjoy Milan." Describing what he arranged in detail.

"Milan, why there?" Questioning him.

"Tory expressed interest in going there. I offered her some funds, told her to enjoy it. Needless to say, she was thrilled," hugging me tightly.

"You did that for me?" I squealed, gushing with happiness.

"I did that for us…." Grabbing me, he pulled me completely on his lap, wrapping my legs around him in his desk chair.

"For five more days, isn't that great?" Pushing his manhood against me, I was happy once again.

I knew the days would pass too quickly, but I felt some relief knowing I didn't have to leave tomorrow.

"Yes, that's great," agreeing with him. Leaning in, he kissed me softly, pulling on my bottom lip, just teasing me enough.

"Now let's be happy." Smiling as he opened my robe. My perky breasts brushed his face, moving in, softly sucking on my nipples, pulling, and licking. I got aroused by his mouth, so did he. Dominique was wearing some stylish lounging gear, so it was easy for him to pull them down with the slightest tug. He maneuvered them with ease while lifting me up and placing me gently on top of his hard tip. I was wet and still a bit nervous about my sexual abilities, so he naturally led me down his shaft with ease. He taught me moves, moves I still use to this day. I rode him as he manipulated my hips, this was new for me, but I liked it. Then it happened, this time so quickly.

"Fuck Allie, you are so tight." Exploding inside of me again. My tight little box made him mad. He loved to devour it. "I promise I will play with you later with my tongue." Dominique needed to have me often. I knew he would keep that promise. He described me as a desert he could not stop having. I was full of semen inside of me, I could feel it dripping out, so I skipped off to the bathroom in his office, "Come back," he laughed.

"I will, promise!" Vowing that I would eventually.

"Who skips? That's too funny," speaking to himself, he was entertained.

"I heard that." As I peeked out of the door.

"I meant it in a good way." Smiling me off.

I went inside the bathroom, cleaned my little parts off, and returned to him.

Tilting his head to the right with a concerned look, "I can't lose you; I have to figure this out and soon, my little angel."

Raising my eyebrows, I smiled. I must have looked my age because he got up, embracing me as if I was his child. Something in Dominique knew that he couldn't keep me locked up in his beautiful world, but he was going to try for as long as he could. The fact that I was on summer break was in my favor. It also helped that he was extremely wealthy and that my mother was a selfish bitch. Tory will want to go back to NYC soon. I knew I didn't have too much time.

Dominique ran a bath for me before dinner. Like everything else in his home, the bathroom was luxurious. White marble everywhere, the room elegant with various sizes of illuminated candles, and rose petals lining my bath. He did this all for my pleasure. The soft sound of Miles Davis playing in the background. I knew this because I studied music for a semester. All alone, I thought, how did I get here? Was I going to wake up and have all of this just be a beautiful dream? I felt unique for the first time in my life, this man was my lifeline to everything.

CHAPTER 10

Charles in Charge

I had finished putting on makeup and doing my hair in an elegant high ponytail, and was wondering what to wear. Having all these high-end designer clothes and not sure what he would like, I was suddenly startled by a thirty-something-year-old man in our bedroom. He spoke with a feminine voice. I quickly realized he was gay.

"Hello, you must be Allie!" Exaggerating his words. "I am Charles," he gave me two fake kisses on my cheeks. I laughed so hard; he was hysterical.

"Hi Charles, it's nice to meet you, but who are you... I mean, what are you doing here in my room?" Asking him nicely. It brought the fairy godmother to a new level.

"I am your new best friend!" Fake flipping his hair, Charles began to explain that he was a stylist, also a dear friend of Dominique's. He followed up by telling me my hair was a "no, no," and said to follow him. Charles had a mission, so I naturally followed him into the master. He unpacked devices for straightening, curling, and tons of products. Everything had a purpose. Charles went into my hair and makeup like I was walking the runway in an hour, and maybe I kind of was. I'd never had this type of personal attention; I felt significant. He was animated and kept me laughing the entire time.

After Charles finished, he proudly spun me around to show the amazing work that he had done.

"Wow, oh my god, you are a genius!" Squealing with excitement.

"Yes, I know, I know, but darling I had a beautiful canvas to work with, this is all you honey!" Singing my praises, even I believed him, I looked like I belonged on the cover of Vogue. My outlook on myself was changing rapidly. I saw myself as elegant and stunning, again another first for me. I felt empowered by my beauty. Oh, how I needed to keep this feeling. Would I be enough for him? My feelings shifted slightly when I thought about losing Dominique. I had to be strong, like Tory and make him want *me* more than I did him.

Charles quickly shuffled me to the bedroom, where he ordered me nicely to try two outfits he had assembled while I was bathing. They were both dresses and both exquisite.

"I say no on the red honey," snapping his fingers with attitude. He put a white dress up against me. "Above the knee and below the thigh, this is it!" Cheering me to get dressed. Charles, my new bestie, chose a semi-short number with a plunging neckline that went further than anything I would ever wear, but long sleeves, so it seemed to all work beautifully. Pairing my dress with simple diamond studs that I didn't know at the time were real, and a Cartier rose gold Love Bracelet. I had always wanted one, but they are costly for a young girl. Lastly, the shoes, he placed a pair of sparkly Jimmy Choo's at my feet. They had multi-colored stones and crystals. Wow, they were absolutely whimsical and sexy in the same breath.

He insisted on snapping a quick photo of me to catalog; I

didn't know what that meant at the time.

"Honey, you should be modeling; you take amazing photographs!" Gushing at his work. I thought to myself, yes, maybe I could.

"No, I'm not like those girls!" Shyly looking down.

"No, you are not; you are better!" Proudly still gushing from his work.

I think Charles knew I was insecure, so he tried to encourage me. I did feel special, so beautiful, my heart was whole. Could this get any better? I'm genuinely a princess in my own life. I looked in the mirror and saw a woman to be loved, not a child.

The formal living room was where I found my love waiting for me, with just a smile and a bottle of rosé Champagne. Looking elegant, he wore a white sport coat, a white shirt with baby blue stripes, and white pants. We matched perfectly.

I thought he was going to drop his glass when he saw me! His mouth was wide open but quickly turned into the most brilliant smile.

"Do you like it?" I asked with a silly grin.

"Yes, my angel, you look confident and stunning!" Stating the truth, or at least it felt like it at the time.

"Really?" Faltering ever so slightly, I still hadn't found my confidence.

Smiling, he shook his head. "My love, of course, you are so fucking beautiful, with or without all of this. I brought Charles here so that you understand just how unearthly you are".

Dissecting it carefully, I agreed with him. I remember this day vividly, but I'm not completely sure this was all for me. I mean I don't think Dominique could have presented me as a sixteen-year-old with just so-so style, but he could present me as a cover girl. I half smile thinking about how little I knew, but that would all change soon.... but not too soon. "I also think it is time for you to transform into a woman, no?"

Dominique asked Charles to take photos of us. Giving him a large envelope before walking him out. Not before Charles gave me his card, an authentic hug, and told me to call him if I ever needed a touch-up or just a friend. Embracing Charles, I said, "yes, of course I will!"

I just had a photograph with this sought out bachelor. It made me feel undeniably important.

CHAPTER 11

A Mediterranean Night

Dominique grabbed the Champagne from the ice. "I thought we would eat here, but this is too stuffy, so let's go outside." Guiding me through two French doors. Outside was also something out of Architectural Design magazine. Dominique had a beautiful table set for us outside on a terrace overlooking the Mediterranean Sea. Candles were everywhere on the small, elegant table and lined the entire terrace, pool, everything. It was something out of a romantic movie where the man proposes. This was much more intimate and romantic for us, he explained. I was thrilled by his surprise; it was such a picturesque view.

Leaping into his arms, I began kissing him. This time my kiss was that of a woman, not a child. I moved slowly, the way he kissed me, with intention. I nibbled on his tongue and moved it around in our mouths. I felt alive, utterly confident in what I was doing. He retaliated, kissing me harder; I felt him growing again. I giggled a little; I made him hard with my kiss. He smiled and laughed as well; he knew the attraction was undeniable between us. I know now that as evil as it sounds, this man was in love with a girl that he camouflaged into a woman.

We sat down, separated slightly. The table was smaller, so we could touch, everything was well thought out. Dominique kissed my forehead and proposed a toast.

"Here's to the biggest surprise of my life, my sweet Allie."

"Thank you," I meant it. "Thank you for all of this." Acknowledging his generosity.

"I mean it, Allie... I'm in love with you. I think I loved you from the moment I looked into your eyes. I see you; I adore you, and I will take care of you so that you don't ever have to be alone again," Dominique conceded as he brushed my face.

"I believe you. I have never believed in anyone until now." My eyes welled up with large pools of tears.

Dominique quickly grabbed me, held me in his arms, so tightly it hurt, yet it felt good knowing he was there for me. I left a mark on his shoulder with my makeup and tried to clean it, but he would have none of that. He took his napkin off his lap, cleaning the makeup from under my eyes. I looked like a baby raccoon, which made us both crack up in laughter.

"Listen, I know this is all new for you, but I will keep you safe; you can trust me. For me, please, my angel, be happy." Holding my face. I believed what he said, but no one ever loved me like this, so doubt was hard to keep at bay.

We dined on fresh fish and vegetables. I was introduced to a lovely white, burgundy wine and just adored the music he chose in French; it was one of the most romantic nights of my life. After dinner, he pulled me to my feet and slowed danced with me, kissing me lightly throughout.

"I have a couple more surprises for you," pointing to my ears.

"Oh, you do, what? Why are you touching my ears, love?"

"Your earrings are real diamonds; they're another birthday gift and the same with the love bracelet, my angel." Whispering in my ear.

"For me? Really... I don't know what to say. They're so extravagant. I'm so grateful, thank you so much, for everything." Jumping up like a girl, kissing him excitedly on the mouth. My tears were gone, and he was the only one to take them away or the only one to put them back. No one actually mattered except for him. He has the power over me to love me or destroy me.

"You... deserve... everything, and I will give it to you." Kissing me between words. I believed everything he said at the time; anything he said was the truth to me. I was a girl in love, and he was a man possessing me. Little did I know how this would shape who I became in my life.

That evening Dominique talked about his siblings and his funny mother, Claire. He said that she was an eccentric lady who liked to throw parties and dance, even if it were just with him and his sisters. They seemed like a very close family full of joy and love, something I only saw at the cinema. The night got late so we retired to our bedroom. We brushed our teeth together while playing in the water. It was pretty childish. Still, he felt comfortable acting immaturely with me because of my age. Quickly his face changed to concern as he pulled me to our bed, sitting us down facing one another.

Staring at me with a worried look, "I never want to share you with anyone. You need to promise me."

I, then for the first time, looked into his eyes with confidence and said, "I will never betray us. I don't want anyone but you. I want to marry you someday."

He was confused by what I had just said, but quickly realized that I pledged myself to him. "Do you really want that? Because I would marry you if I could tomorrow. Unfortunately, I cannot until you are 17 years old, when you are legal in the United States."

I knew he meant what he said, and I was ready to marry him today. Embracing him while kissing his muscular chest that was pressing against me, I felt an overwhelming desire, and expressed my longing for him, but before I could even finish what I was saying, he was showing me just how much he wanted me through his erection. I felt it against my leg. We couldn't make love enough; a good night quickly turned to him wanting to lick my "special little spot." He had taken my virginity; this must have turned him on daily. For the very first time, I knew it was okay to feel something for a guy. "I fucking love him so much, with everything in my body." I began to ache for him now. He touched me with his fingers, exploring deep within my pussy; he understood I was his and would be for as long as he wanted. We made passionate love that night like a couple, more so than the previous times. We had a harmonious rhythm and made sounds together like we were lovers forever.

After we finished, we laid entwined.

"I did *not* see this coming…" confessing as he rubbed my back.

"I did," returning his touch with mine. We were fully content.

I fell asleep with my head buried in his chest and woke the same way, tucked nicely in his arms. Dominique looked at me with the most incredible smile, "I had a dream, but I realized it wasn't a dream because you're right here." I think back, was this the happiest time for me? Yes, most likely, I just wish that I could sometimes be as naïve as then. If only love could be that easy.

Rock the Boat Baby

Dominique amazed me with a beautiful boat ride. Low anc behold, my prince had a "small yacht" as well. Now I'm really in fairytale land for sure.

"Get dressed, my angel. We are heading for the sea!"

He had swimsuits hanging in the closet like a department store magically delivered just for me. I grabbed a black basic Brazilian bottom bikini and a loose-fitting long white cover-up. I entered the kitchen with no makeup and a messy French braided, mohawk ponytail. I had seen a famous actress wear her hair like this and now, at last, had the confidence to wear it.

"You look beautiful, different now without make-up, you've grown into your own, you walk with a walk now, look at you and your hair...super!" Bragging like a proud boyfriend.

"Why, thank you, kind sir! I feel terrific." Smiling as I bit into a juicy apple. After I tossed it playfully to him, he bit off a piece and quickly kissed my lips with the wetness from the fruit.

We left the house and went to a nearby marina in town. We approached the dock, and Dominique explained that the yacht was substantially smaller than the others, measuring thirty-eight meters. I thought it was anything but. We were greeted by a small group of staff in white uniforms. He was polite and introduced his crew to me as his girlfriend. I was shocked yet so thrilled to hear the man of my dreams announce to someone other than me that I was somebody, let alone a girlfriend. We took a quick tour and then shoved off to the open water. French chill music played in the background as we lay on a daybed, soaking up the beautiful sun. A small girl named Ingrid approached us and asked to speak to Dominique about the menu. He excused himself to discuss our meal plan. Returning to our lounge, and laying towards me, I followed his lead. Leaning in to kiss me, we were interrupted.

"Excusez-moi, monsieur," Ingrid said while clearing her throat. She'd arrived back with a glistening bottle of white wine.

"Merci, laissez-le, je vais l'ouvrir," dismissing her nicely, and then turning to me.

Dominique loved to educate, explaining the Chablis wine we were about to drink. "Citrus and white flower aromas with dry, lean, light-bodied flavors. It's as perfect as the hot sunny day that we are having." Explaining to me while swirling his glass. I loved hearing him speak. Anything he had to say was intriguing and worldly. After describing the wine, he asked me to smell it, so I did what he asked. It had a very different smell than the Champagne I had been drinking, but I very much liked this foreign scent. I would later in life marry into the wine industry. I believe this is another point in Dominique's favor in my heart of hearts. Dominique took a small sip of the wine after smelling it.

"Delicious, my angel, please now you try." Signaling with his hand. I took a bigger sip than he did, making him laugh. "No, darling, savor the taste. You are like a baby bird hungry to be fed. You are so funny little one." Kissing my lips softly as I giggled in his mouth. He loved my innocence and playfulness, which might have been lacking in previous women in his life or in general because God knows I wasn't one of those yet. Years later, I too realized this was a tool in helping a man stay very interested... They needed to feel young.

He put the wine glass down while grabbing the back of my neck, pulling me into him for a long and delicious kiss. I could taste the wine in his mouth and smell it on his breath. It was intoxicating in so many ways. He took a piece of ice from the bucket and began to tease my nipples through my suit. This was an obvious first for me. I enjoyed the coldness of the ice melting in his mouth as he held onto my hot, subtle breasts. He saw my reaction and wanted to do more for me. I could see the hunger in his eyes. It grew like an animal that found its prey.

"Close your eyes, Allie, let me explore you a bit. Feel, don't see." Whispering in his sensual French accent. I did as he instructed. I closed my eyes; I had no choice; he was a god before me. I heard his hands in the ice bucket, but I didn't know where the ice would go next. My anticipation grew.

I felt his hands quickly pull my bottoms off, and within a couple of seconds, his cold, wet mouth was between my legs. The ice moving around. It was like nothing I could imagine. What was this man doing to me? Why did it feel so good? I was so turned on that I began to move my body softly with urges to scream "I love this," but I kept the cries in my head a while longer. Dominique continued to please me until the ice was gone. All that was left was his mouth. It was no longer cool; it was like an oven on me. He engulfed my pussy, licking deep

61

inside of me; he wanted to please. Pushing on my clit while using his fingers deeply on the inside and outside in perfect harmony with his mouth. He would not let up; he could feel my body grind away. I was close and then closer, on edge. I had to speak. I screamed out his name, "Dominique, oh Dominique!" I came hard all over his pleasing face.

I laid there, limp, waiting for him to speak, my eyes still closed. I felt him crawling up my entire body. He was at my face; I could feel his breath. He began kissing me deeply. His lips were wet from my pussy, full of raging passion. "Open your eyes, my love." I did with a pleasing smile. "I need you to know you're mine. I fucking need you, Allie. Please give it to me. I have to have you," Crying out as he entered me slowly. Holding on tightly as he pushed deep inside of me. I was dripping, which made him ravines. Kissing me as he moved further inside of me, over and over thrusting me until he couldn't take one more stroke. "I'm going to cum, angel, I'm going to cum inside of you! Oh, fuck!" Pushing one last time, I could feel him release inside of me. We were completely content and fell asleep with him inside of me. I was becoming a woman ahead of my time. Was this in my favor? I don't know, possibly. I was alive for the first time. It definitely shaped my love-making skills, this I know as the truth.

Later that day, Dominique decided it was a night for music. "Allie, how would you like to go into town this evening?" Asking me was like asking a child if they wanted to go to a fair. "Yes, of course, I would love to," Flashing him a big smile. "Great angel, why don't you take some time now for yourself. Ingrid will come and assist you in any fashion you should need," looking towards Ingrid, he nodded.

"Bien sûr Monsieur Chirac, avec plaisir." Agreeing with pleasure, she followed me. Dominique had a commanding presence, yet he was still quite kind in his approach. The people who worked for him deeply admired him; you could see it.

I grabbed a glass of Chablis and headed to the master bedroom. I began to look through my closet, where all my lovely clothes were unpacked and put away neatly. I really felt like I would burst when I walked into the vast space that was all mine. Ingrid followed me in and waited for my instructions. Ingrid was a young French girl, no more than twenty, tiny stature, a very simple and fresh-faced blonde. It felt good to have her, someone that knew St. Tropez a bit. I asked her about the nightlife, what the women were like and how they dressed. I must have rattled on for half an hour. Ingrid felt relaxed and told me all I needed to know.

"I would appreciate your opinion between a couple of things," I said as I pulled out two dresses.

"With pleasure!" Smiling on, Ingrid was happy to be involved. We mulled over the shoes, how to wear my hair and makeup. It was my first girlfriend-like moment here, so it was really nice to have someone young to speak to.

Tory never really wanted to help me with anything, not even a tampon when I got my period. I felt confident in my choices having Ingrid with me on this night. Ingrid tended to me with ease and grace, pouring wine and playing with my hair. I really grew fond of her, but I knew that this was a friendship behind closed doors only. I knew that Dominique would not have me befriending the staff, but for now, this was close enough to a friend for me.

I came to the main deck, where beautiful, white sofas lined the center of the space. My eyes followed Dominique; he was on the phone conducting some sort of business and seemed quite upset over a deal he was making. It was the first time I had heard or witnessed him angry. His tone swiftly left his voice as he caught a glimpse of me in the corner of his eye.

"Allie," he let out a great sigh. "Is it possible that you could get any more beautiful? Absolument magnifique!" Walking towards me, pulling my hands away from my body to get a complete look at what I was wearing. I pleased him, and I liked it.

I decided that evening with the help of Ingrid that I would wear a gold, silk lamé, bodycon, Dolce & Gabbana dress. It had a ruche design with shoulder straps, so it was just sexy enough, but not too much as to maintain its elegance. I paired it with a taupe 100 mm, Jonatina sandal by Christian Louboutin. If you know Louboutin, they are anything but sandals. I knew it looked amazing on, but I didn't realize just how until I got confirmation from my lover.

"I couldn't be prouder; you make me so happy, angel." Picking me up off my feet, kissing me with his soft, full lips. His smell was divine, a mix of his own masculinity and cologne, a heavenly scent that was creating a chemical reaction from me. I was high on this man's smell. I didn't know at the time that this was a pheromone thing. His scent was all-consuming. Kissing me lightly so as not to mess up my pretty lipstick, after all, he wanted me to stay fresh for the exciting evening he had planned for us.

"Let's have a glass of wine or Champagne before we leave... which would you prefer?" Dominique held up two bottles.

"Anything you decide is fine," I answered back, still with the hesitation of a girl.

"Angel, you decide. What would you like?" Dominique teased me about being confident. "Alright then, I would love to have something different, maybe a fancy cocktail in a Martini glass?" Replying with conviction.

"Done! Ingrid, what can you make Allie that resembles her description?" Dominique spoke to Ingrid for a few minutes longer. I don't think he really wanted her opinion; he knew what he would have her make. He walked back to me with his Scotch, and a Martini glass filled with a peach-colored substance. He called it a 007. I was so excited; it was exactly what I imagined I wanted. Fruity, smooth and didn't taste like alcohol. It was deliciously yummy. I later came to find it was Vodka, Peach Schnapps, and Seven-Up. We finished our drinks and left the mega yacht. The boat didn't have a name, I asked why as we were leaving, and he said he didn't want to name it until he came up with the perfect one. I thought this was odd, but I didn't know either way how the naming of a boat went.

The yachts bordered the main street in St. Tropez. It was all very glamorous. The onlookers lined the boats to take photographs in hopes of seeing someone famous. This is what Ingrid had told me earlier in my room. I felt like a princess because he made me feel like this. I was transforming, and I didn't even realize just how much. We had several people in the crowd snap photos of us as we exited the boat. Pictures of me, why I thought? Dominique turned to me as if he could read my thoughts.

"They think you're famous, my love," he smiled.

"No, they must be looking at you." Claiming the truth.

"Allie, Allie... you are a funny girl." Leaning down to kiss my hand. We walked along the busy St. Tropez streets with a tall, white, maybe fifty, very serious man in tow. He was our bodyguard, Andre. I guess looking back at it, he didn't want anyone to get too close to us. I liked it because it made us look important. Little did I know just how important this Dominique was.

CHAPTER 13

My Green-Eyed Devil

"This is the place, my love, we are here, Opera restaurant," Dominique held me closely. I looked in amazement. This place was so spectacular. We walked up a small set of stairs; the enormous security guard shook his hand and welcomed us. A small, very polished, older French woman ran over to him, kissing his cheeks quickly, and then turned to me to do the same. She was thrilled to see us and promptly took us into the outdoor garden restaurant and cabaret show. The entire room was white, except for the stage. The house was full of sexy women performing a risqué dance on a catwalk in the center of the room. Twinkling lights and loud music in the trees, but not interrupting conversations throughout the room. It had around 25 tables in it, and off to the left was a U-shaped bar, with what appeared to be single people socializing. Later in my life, when I returned to St. Tropez, I found out that Opera was the most exclusive place to go to in the summer.

The French woman was the maîtres' and introduced herself as the Queen of the Night. She made us laugh when she spoke about the length of time she knew Dominique. Leaning in my ear, she said, "I've never seen him bring a lady here. He must really love you." I blushed and smiled. Dominique was so proud of me. As we walked, his hand guided the small of my back to keep me close to him. I was his actual girlfriend, and I was special. I felt it from him, and all the others in the room confirmed it, the whispers from the ladies around our table.

"They are all wondering who you are, angel," smiling and waving to a few onlookers. I shook my head and kissed his hand. The kiss must have sealed his heart because I kissed it like he was royalty, and he melted at the sight of it.

We had a table next to the catwalk of seductive ladies performing. It was like something I had never seen; provocatively witty. Dominique shook Felix, the head waiter's hand. Felix was pleased to see Dominique. Dominique had a way of noticing people and respecting the staff, treating them like they mattered, another quality that made me feel proud to be with him. He told Felix to start "the princess" with her new favorite 007, and he would have a Hendrick's gin Martini.

Felix joked, "yes, Mr. Bond." Dominique found it amusing, but I most certainly saw him as a James Bond character. After our drinks, he ordered the best vintage Dom Perignon rosé Champagne. It was so rich and perfect with the Russian caviar and oysters we had to start. Then he ordered a special bottle of wine called a Montrachet. He described the white wine as perfect to pair with our fresh sea bass and root vegetables.

At the beginning of the night, Dominique asked me if I had a preference for food, but I would shyly ask him to take care of all of it, that he was the expert. Being schooled would later benefit me in so many ways. This was the theme throughout our dinners. I was speed lea rning about food and wine, sex, love, everything, and I couldn't have been a more willing participant. Before the main course came, I excused myself to use the lady's room. As I walked through the room, I could feel the many men staring at me. I felt noticed, and it made me smile to have the attention of those good looking guys. I must have caught the eye of one in particular because he followed behind me to ask if we knew one another.

"Bonjour belle. On s'est pas déjà rencontrés…Paris, Monaco, ici peut-être?" The young man asked. I could never forget him. He was extremely good looking, maybe around 25. As tall as Dominique, but nothing like him otherwise. He had black hair and green eyes, just like me. It was odd, but he felt familiar like we might know one another, possibly in another life.

"No, I have never met you in any of those places." Dismissing him. I thought this was the right thing to do.

"Oh, you're American! Ok, so am I. You understand French though?" Coming on strong, the handsome stranger replied.

"Oui merci, I am American," I half smiled. It was hard to not smile; he was so easy to look at.

"It is a pleasure to make your acquaintance. I'm Raphael Vega, my friends call me Raph, and you are?" Extending his hand, but I did not take it. He may have had a beautiful smile, but I was cautious.

"Nice to meet you, Raph, but I'm here with someone," dismissing him, yet in a flirty nature.

"That is a funny name," laughing under his breath. I couldn't help but join him in a laugh at my stand-offish comment.

"I'm sorry, that was kind of rude. My name is Allie, but you'll have to excuse me. Nice to meet you, Raph!" Quickly leaving for the lady's bathroom. I could hear him in the background, "Yes, pretty Allie, hope to see you again."

He was gone when I came out, and I was slightly relieved that he was. I felt like I was betraying Dominique by speaking to the handsome stranger, yet part of me looked for him when I walked the long walk to my table. There was something about him, I don't know, a sense of familiarity.

Dominique stood up, "Are you ok, Allie?" Questioning with deep concern.

"Yes, I am fine. Why?" Answering under my breath. My love was seemingly a bit miffed. "I saw you speaking to a man when I looked for you. Who was he? Someone you knew?"

He waited for me to answer with such a look, a look I had never seen, that of jealousy. I had upset him, and now my face became hot. I was noticeably nervous.

"I, um, I don't know him, no. He just stopped me to ask if we had met in Monaco before. I said no, and that's it, I went to the bathroom." I stressed in a shaky voice.

"Hey, it's ok angel, I was just worried that he was bothering you. I am not upset with you at all. I'm just protective." Pulling me to him, kissing my forehead, I felt relieved and also guilty. Did he see my eyes light up from the attention of another man? Would this be the start of what is to come in my life?

My thoughts were all over, and he could see it.

We finished our bottle of wine, and both decided to skip

dessert. Saying our goodbyes to the lovely French lady and others that Dominique knew at the tables surrounding us. Dominique was well connected and most certainly an important man, so it took a while before we could get through the crowd. We got to the exit with our bodyguard in tow and stepped out into the busy street. I heard a familiar voice from earlier in the evening.

"Have a beautiful night, Allie baby!" It was Raph and a fellow mate of his. I did a quick wave-off, but that wouldn't cut it with Dominique.

"What can we help you with?" Pointing his finger at Raph, he yelled out.

"Nothing, sir, I wasn't talking to you." Sarcastically he goaded him.

Dominique did not fare well with this. He went to Raph, chest to chest, "You should be schooled; she's with me and doesn't want to talk to you." Dominique was a strong man with a worthy adversary, Raph. I stepped to Dominique, a bit frightened at this point, shaking from fear.

"Please, Dominique, let's go back to the boat, please, love." By this time, our bodyguard had got between them. Dominique's eyes met mine, and he realized how scared I was. "Yes, angel, let's go. I'm sorry, don't be upset."

Apologizing again, we walked away. I was frightened and way too young to handle all of what was going on. We walked away; I was thankful that he didn't turn back. I could hear Raph taunting him as we walked away. Raph knew precisely what he was doing, but I, on the other hand, did not. This was my first look at jealousy in regard to me. I had only seen men get that way with my mother, I was now beginning to see it firsthand, and I didn't like it, at least not till years later when I found ways of using it to my benefit.

There was tension in the air as we walked in silence to the boat. As we crossed the small bridge onto the yacht, Dominique asked me softly If I was ok. I didn't answer. I took my heels off and walked to the sofas; Dominique followed closely behind. We sat together; it was a beautiful evening. I had hoped that it would not be spoiled because of me.

"I'm so sorry, I didn't tell you that I shared my name with that stranger. Forgive me for leaving it out. I just didn't want to upset you; you seemed so concerned. I never thought, I mean I never wanted that to happen, I love you." Blubbering an apology.

"Allie, I am not upset with you, the guy was fucking with me, and I let him. I was jealous, he is a younger, good-looking guy, and you smiled at him. It made me fucking crazy!" Explaining as he held my face in his strong hands. "I love you! I don't want you to be with anyone else." Kissing me desperately. Dominique filled my mouth with his tongue. It felt hungry. I could taste the alcohol, and I was quickly aroused by his desire to own me. I made him jealous, me Allie, the girl that no one ever noticed, has this gorgeous man losing his shit. I was delirious with desire. I needed to have him as much as he did me.

Dominique told the staff to leave us for the remainder of the night, walking back to me while taking off his shirt. I couldn't wait to touch his chest and six-pack, so smooth, hard, and tan from the summer sun. With his athletic form, Dominique gently picked me up into his arms. I reached high on my toes to kiss his chiseled frame. He slowly turned me around. I landed back on my feet as he unzipped my dress. I was wearing nothing underneath, and he was pleasantly surprised.

"Fuck Allie, you went without panties, and you didn't tell me? You little devil, now you are making me even crazier." Speaking in a low, sexy voice. I was standing with my back to him as he pushed into me while pulling my dress down, allowing it to fall to the floor. I could hear him unbuttoning his pants and taking them down. I felt how hard he was as he brushed my lower back; I was hot for him and couldn't wait to kiss him again. He nibbled on my neck, turning me around once again back to him. One brute move while picking me up, ordering me to wrap my legs around him. I did as he commanded. My lover was still engulfed with anger from the end of the night. He needed to have me, to own me.

He laid me down on my back and, quickly without care, slid his hard cock deep inside me. I was dripping wet, it hurt, but I liked it. Dominique was filled with rage and passion as he drove his long rod in and out of my small pussy. Instructing me to touch myself simultaneously. I didn't understand, so he guided me like a good teacher. This was amazing. I had played with myself before, but never with a man. I could not contain my happiness; I was so into it. He kept at me, driving harder and faster.

"Don't do that again. I was so jealous. You're mine, Allie!" Telling me over and over, the more he spoke, the harder he pushed. His cock was ready to explode, and so was I. Our bodies were synchronized. I was overwhelmed with lust and his desire to possess me.

"My love, I am going to cum... now!" I let out whimpers of emotion.

"Allie, oh Allie, you're killing me, baby...I'm cumming with you, angel!" Crying out in ecstasy, he collapsed. This was raw and emotional, something I had never experienced. I made him lose it, and I liked it.

Dominique soon turned tender. He carried me to bed, laying me gently down while brushing my hair from my face. He spoke about us, telling me that he would figure out our next step in our future. I wasn't sure what he could do because I was still a girl legally, no matter how many pairs of heels I would put on. I trusted he could and would do anything to keep us together.

The next morning Dominique was sitting inside at his desk. I was restless, and he had to take a few calls for work, so he suggested I take his credit card and go shopping. "Andre will go with you." He directed towards me while speaking loud enough for our massive bodyguard to hear. Andre nodded and waited for me.

"Dominique, I don't need him to go with me. Nothing is going to happen." Pleading, I felt like I could change his mind.

"I don't know, Allie... last night... I just want to keep you safe." Dominique was overly concerned.

"Come on, I'm fine for a couple of hours and no offense, but I don't need a big guy following me around. That will only bring more attention to me." Pleading my case one last time.

"Ok, but this is against my better judgment." Reluctantly, he agreed.

"Great!" Kissing him, I ran to change.

"Ingrid, please go with her in town." He ordered. I didn't care. Girl's day was exactly what I wanted.

Saint Tropez, the small and ultra-rich village on the French Riviera. The cobbled streets, filled with tiny fashion boutiques, cafes, and restaurants. I zig-zagged through and bought a pair of shoes, a silk scarf, and some French perfume. I even bought Ingrid a bag but asked her not to reveal it to anyone, we laughed, and she agreed. She was the closest thing I had here to a friend, and I was super grateful. Ingrid suggested a small restaurant, off the beaten path, on a hidden street in a "more eclectic shopping area" that she knew about. Explaining to me that most tourists didn't know about this hidden Italian gem. I loved exploring in a foreign place. This was a whole new experience for me. We came upon this quaint brick establishment with large windows and one small door that led into the restaurant. It only housed twenty seats. They only had long tables and benches to share, so you had to sit and occupy the table with strangers. It was quaint and smelled of the most delicious firewood oven pizza. We drank wine and ate pizza and shared salads. It was unsophisticated but perfect. I enjoyed the normalcy of it all, chatting with the owner and others at our table.

What I didn't expect in this place was what I got.

"Hello, Allie baby!" The once again familiar voice called out to me. Raph, the handsome and oh-so cocky guy from Opera last night. Oh no, what the hell.

"Hello, troublemaker," looking at him with contempt, trying to hide my smile. "Can you excuse me, Ingrid," I stood, pulling his arm aside. "Why did you try and befriend me and then start that fight with my boyfriend?" Demanding he answer.

"I'm sorry, Allie, I was drinking too much, and he seems like an asshole, the way he fronts himself. You look like his puppet. I think you deserve better." Raph ranted on. What did he know? Nothing about Dominique; he only sees the flash.

"Listen, you are not my father. I don't know you! I'm no one's puppet. So, please stay away from me!" I turned away to sit down, but Raph grabbed my arm, and I turned to him once again.

"Listen, I'm sorry. I don't know, I just liked you immediately when I saw you. That isn't a line Allie. There's something between us. I think you feel it too." Confessing as he searched for confirmation. I listened. How could I not have some attraction to him, he was so hot, and his eyes were penetrating. I really liked Raph for some reason. I didn't want to be angry. I actually felt drawn to him too, as much as I didn't want to admit it, he got to me.

"Raph, there is nothing here. Trust me, nothing." Pulling his hand away returning to my seat. I didn't believe my own words, but I wasn't going to encourage him. He left. I wondered if I would ever see him again. I was freaking out. I begged Ingrid not to mention anything, she agreed to keep quiet. I prayed that she would.

Dominique eagerly awaited my return with an afternoon drink, an Aperol spritz, describing it as a light cocktail, perfect for a beautiful, mid-afternoon summer day. He asked me to show him what I had purchased. I said yes and that I would return in a few.

"Oh love, your credit card is in my bag. You can grab it out of the side pocket!" I yelled, walking down the steps. Dominique smiled at my innocence; most girls would have never mentioned the card. He opened up my baby blue Hermes Birkin bag that he had graciously given me for my birthday. He pulled out his black American Express card. He also discovered another card in my bag.

When I returned, I passed Ingrid, "I'm so sorry, Allie, he questioned me, and I can't lose my job." She remorsefully explained. Oh no, what did she do? I returned to Dominique wearing a bright yellow, flowery sundress that I intended to model for him.

"Allie, what is this?" Dominique asked while holding up a white business card with gold lettering that said "Raphael Edouard-Shae." I was in shock. My head was racing. How did that get in my bag?

My mouth fell open, and I spoke, "Dominique, I didn't put

that there, I swear."

"Did you see this guy today?" Questioning me like a child with his arms crossed. I knew he was fuming; I could see his body language cold and unloving. My palms began to sweat, I panicked, and I couldn't breathe.

"I did, I bumped into him... It wasn't planned...at lunch. We spoke for a minute...enough for me to tell him he was completely out of line." I couldn't control my stammer; I was feeling dizzy.

"Allie, are you ok?" Dominique was seemingly concerned now. I began to fall, and then there was nothing.

I awoke confused, laying in my bed in the master suite. "What happened?"

"You fainted, angel," stroking my hair and cheek, my love was by my side. I tried to sit up, but he pushed me lightly back down. "Ingrid brought you some orange juice; this will help." Dominique was concerned for my health. He was visibly upset with himself for overreacting about the card. "Allie, please forgive me. Ingrid explained what happened at the restaurant. That kid must have dropped his card in your bag when you turned to sit down. I don't know what is wrong with me... how I could accuse you!" He was angry with himself.

"It's ok, as long as you believe me. I would never betray you. I love you more than anything.... you are my world... you are everything!" My voice cracked as my eyes filled with tears that couldn't be stopped. Sobbing in his arms as he stroked my hair,

I was so scared of losing him. Would he throw me away? I cried harder.

"Allie, please don't; you are breaking my heart. I can't have you sad, my angel." Begging while wiping away my tears and kissing my mouth. His kiss got more profound, and so did his thirst for his young lover. He stared into me. "Angel, I need you; I love you, and I'm sorry for not trusting you. I promise this person will never show his face again. Can I make love to you, Allie?"

He consoled me with his mouth. I nodded yes; I knew sex would bring us close again. I wanted him and his love back. I laid back and gazed at him, my beautiful man, how I longed for him inside of me, to make it all better again. He opened my dress and pulled his pants just over his ass, enough to push inside of me. We didn't speak as he entered me deeply. We only kissed. It was our bonding again. Everything was better than before.

I had fallen asleep for a while but woke to my darling tickling my nose.

"What are you doing?" I smiled, slowly opening my eyes.

"Wake up, sleeping beauty, you've been out for hours... I have a surprise for you."

"I'm awake, I'm awake.... What kind of surprise !?" Rubbing my eyes like a kitten.

"We are heading to Monaco now. Come!" Dominique

eagerly pulled me to my feet and brought me to the upper deck. It appeared we had already left St. Tropez and were on the open waters. Wow, this is crazy. We are heading to Monte-Carlo, the playground for the ultrawealthy. What could be better?

CHAPTER 14

Monaco

My love needed to educate me on our next stop. The global sensation that is the playground of the "rich and famous; Monaco." Dominique explained that Monaco is a sovereign city-state, country, and microstate principality, ruled by a royal family. The head of this family is Prince Albert. He also explained that there are four quarters in Monaco and the one that made it most famous is Monte-Carlo. I was well informed but still, a bit confused by it all. I had, like everyone else, heard about Monte-Carlo. The rumors of opulence, cars, hookers, and Russian billionaires. It sounded fascinating, not that New York City wasn't, but this was an exotic place for me. Located on the French Riviera, where the weather is almost always lovely, it resembled paradise in my mind.

We made our way into the marina in Monte-Carlo. This time we parked our yacht further on the outskirts of the port. This was where the larger vessels were docked. Also, a place where there were no onlookers, unlike St. Tropez, this was a very discreet place, hidden behind a long driveway and security gate. Dominique seemed to enjoy the privacy more than the loud people and cameras of St. Tropez. Me, I didn't care either way. As long as I was by his side, I was content. The country was tiny, yet the world's socialites and oligarchs would pile into this little gem. Dominique divulged stories of the royals and how he got to meet the famous "Prince Albert of Monaco." He told me about the star-studded nightclubs, Jimmy'z and Sass, and his favorite steak restaurant, Beefbar. Dominique booked us into the five-star Hotel L'Hermitage so that he could spoil us with the spa and designer shops. I loved this place already, and I had not even stepped foot off the boat.

Excusing himself to make a call while I fantasized about what the night would hold, as I got increasingly more excited to get dressed for it. I asked Ingrid if she would help me this evening, and she agreed. Barely containing myself, I couldn't wait to see this famous wonderland on the Mediterranean Sea. I only read about this place, now to be here, it was honestly mind-blowing. Me, Allie Hart, jet setter, and a girlfriend to this world-class man.... fucking amazing.

Dominique seemed intense on the phone. I could read his body language outside on the front of the deck, I wondered who he was talking to, but I knew it was probably in my best interest to leave it for now. I left and went to prepare for the evening with Ingrid in tow.

"Ingrid, tell me about Monaco, please," I asked, placing my arm around her shoulder as we walked into the master cabin.

"Well, it's different from St. Tropez, it's made up mostly of millionaires and billionaires, it's the second smallest country in the world. The wealthiest people on the planet live here. They also import their luxury sports cars here: Ferrari's, Lamborghini's, McLaren's, Rolls Royce... You won't just see a few, but hundreds, it's ridiculous Allie!" Ingrid was quite animated when she spoke in her French accent.

I giggled, jumping into my bed, pulling Ingrid down with me, "Tell me more, please. How do they dress?" I whined while playing with her hair.

"Well, it's everything in between...you can dress in a full-length gown or mini, or jeans with designer sneakers, but you should always have a great watch and some diamonds." Animated as she explained in detail. It sounded opulent and eccentric, and I couldn't wait to be a part of it. Ingrid stood up quickly. Feeling awkward from being so relaxed, she snapped to her duties as my assistant. I was okay with that; I actually wanted the help now, and I was getting used to being spoiled. We went into my closet to examine what I had bought in St. Tropez.

"I think you should wear this." Ingrid smiled with a huge grin. She had picked out a black satin, halter, maxi Balmain dress with a slit up the leg. It was elegant, yet very sexy.... just enough sex to make me undeniably a woman! I looked at my earrings and decided on a delicate flower pair. I had picked them up from the Bulgari boutique. The excellent emerald I had got from my Dominique for my special birthday. I might have been extremely young, but I was beginning to understand just how powerful beauty and knowledge of this world could be. So, the grooming began, as I filled my head with possibilities.

Dominique entered the room and announced himself.

"Hello, any little angels in this room?"

Ingrid excused herself, and it was just the two of us.

"I'm in here, Dominique!" I was excited to see him. It felt

like we were apart for days. I ran in his arms, kissing him furiously. He laughed and then began to reciprocate with intensity.

"I missed you, my love!" Kissing his chest through his unbuttoned shirt.

"Hmm, Allie, please, I have to go run out... I'm sorry, I will be back in an hour. We can continue this after dinner. Ok, my angel? I have to jump into a cold shower now!" Rushing away, he left me frustrated.

"Where are you going?" I chirped into the master bathroom.

"I have to see a friend quickly over a Scotch, he's leaving this evening, and I don't want to invite him to dinner," Dominique explained through the shower door.

"Yes, that's fine. I will get ready for tonight... I have a special dress for this evening, can't wait to show you." I muttered to myself while reentering my closet.

"Allie." Dominique sang out in the bathroom.

"Yes, love?" I peeked in the bathroom.

"I love you, angel," he professed, cleaning the steam off the shower revealing his face. I loved him so much, I wanted to scream. I walked over to the door and kissed the shower glass. His lips met mine on the other side.

"I love you!" I opened the door to give him my lips in person.

"Damn, Allie, you make me so happy!" As he pulled me in the shower fully clothed, kissing me passionately. So turned on by this Adonis, grabbing his manhood, I began to stroke it.

"I'm never getting out of here if you continue to touch me, young lady... now out." Hard as a rock, he gently pushed me out of the shower. "Angel, get ready, and I will be back in two hours." His voice echoed.

"On it... tease!" Joking as I exited wet from our kiss. My head was spinning. I couldn't wait to get out and see this mysterious place.

I thought nothing of where he was going until he didn't come back for two hours.

Where was he? I was a bit concerned. He didn't answer his phone or text me. I found Ingrid on the deck and sent her for a glass of white wine, trying Dominique again on my cell. Oh no, I heard his phone ringing, he must have forgotten it. Seeing all of the missed calls on the home page, it was locked but revealed the last callers. I was on the call list five times, and to my surprise, there was another name that he forgot to mention, a woman's name... Jolie. Who is this, Jolie? I became upset and drank my wine fast to soothe my anxiety, but unfortunately, that didn't work. Waiting, I gulped another wine. Now it was going on three hours, and by this time, it was 8 o'clock. Where was he? Was he with this woman? Oh, fuck it, instead of getting upset, I gave him the benefit of the doubt. Left him a note telling him that I would go to L'Hermitage to have a drink. I'm a young lady, and I don't need to be tapping my foot. I should be adventurous and explore a bit. Monaco was at my feet, and I wanted to see some of it. I told the staff where I wanted to go, and they arranged to have a Mercedes taxi pick me up.

Amazed by this palace of a hotel, L'Hermitage. I mean, really…I couldn't believe the richness of it all. Marble everywhere in this grandiose lobby, including the long hall to the bar, full of the same, lined with period mirrors. I got a bit melancholy for a second, thinking about Dominique. The fact that he disappeared without his phone or me. That quickly dissolved when I entered the stunning bar and lounge full of gorgeous people. I walked into a small bar adorned with cut-glass chandeliers and staff all in white, gloves, and tuxedos. It was truly a scene from Cinderella, except I was alone without my prince. I quickly had the attention of all of the waiters and the crowd that was in the room whispering as they watched me enter.

"Bonsoir Mademoiselle," the small French waiter greeted me.

"Bonsoir Monsieur. Table pour deux s'il vous plaît." I requested a table for two. I hoped that Dominique would not leave me alone too long, but it was a curious adventure for now.

"Oui, suivez moi Mademoiselle," the waiter asked me to follow him. I walked through the room gracefully, I felt substantial, and by the crowd's reaction, I could see that it was true. I stood tall at 5'9", but I had an additional four inches this evening, which made me over six feet. I might as well have been sixteen feet tall. My confidence exuded entering the swank spot.

My waiter brought me to a lovely corner table, a rich floral banquet seat, and a white velvet high back chair next to it. I was hoping Dominique would come and wanted to save the chair for him. I ordered a glass of rosé Champagne from the waiter in French, thrilling to use what I had learned in private school, yet never ever dreamed I would be using it in Monte-Carlo. It was all-consuming, me in this lovely place alone, and for the first time, I felt comfortable solo in a room full of strangers. I felt like I belonged. I was coming into my own.

I finished my Champagne and decided to have one more before going back to the boat. As I was ordering another, there he was! How the hell could this be? Standing in the entrance, Raph, the hot, studly twenty-something-year-old, who had caused such a commotion in my life in St. Tropez! Part of me wanted to run, but the intrigued side wanted him to notice that I was here. Craving the way, he would naturally make me smile with his silly banter. I liked the attention of another man. What was happening to me?

Raph took notice immediately. He quickly strutted towards me. I felt warm and overwhelmed, I wanted to hide under the table, but I obviously couldn't. He was drop-dead gorgeous; I was turned on by my fear of getting caught. His statuesque frame in the middle of the room was the center of the world for me right now.

"If it isn't the most beautiful girl on the Riviera... Allie, hello sweet Allie!" Calling out with a devilish and ever so beautiful smile.

"What are you following me now?!" I couldn't hold back my smile.

"What if I said yes?" Pushing his flowing black hair out of his face, he teased.

"Then I would have to call the police because I have a stalker!" Biting my lip as I continued to flirt. I really liked him, he was immature, more like me, yet you could tell he was well-traveled. I was merely acting like I was. There was something so playful and steamy about him. He just oozed sex.

"You're here alone?" Questioning me with a smile that would not leave his beautifully chiseled face. Why does he have to look so good? I want to wrap my legs around his face so severely... Can he read me?

"Yes, for now! I expect my boyfriend any minute, so please don't stand here. I don't want a scene again." Way too much information because he ate that right up.

"Oh! So he was pissed off at you, not just me!" He goaded me.

"You are a naughty boy; you love this, don't you?" Pointing out the obvious. By this time, he had been at my table for more than a minute, and I felt my excitement growing. I had this crazy desire to kiss him. Part of me felt terrible like I was cheating on my love, but the other part of me didn't give a fuck.

My consciousness did not get the better of me; my body involuntarily stood up, "Would you like to join me for a drink?" I couldn't believe the words fell from my, ever so, red lips.

"I would love to. Never thought you would ask; I was

beginning to get tired of standing above you." Laughing as he pulled the chair away and joined me on the sofa. I was surprised, no, shocked, that he didn't sit in the chair, nervous from his proximity, yet all thoughts of Dominique left me while I sat with Raph.

Talking with him for over forty minutes flew by about his life, and mine. Ironically enough, we both lived in New York City. Little did he know that I was sixteen and in school in the Upper Eastside of Manhattan at an all-girls "private" school. He tried to pry, and I was vague about my life at first, only sharing that I lived with my mother alone on Central Park in the Upper East. He was a downtown guy, Tribeca.

Raph had a way about him, asking me all sorts of questions that no-one actually ever did. We spoke about everything, even my secret love of art. I never told anyone I painted, often alone as a child and teenager, but I told *him* about it and even my grandmother Eve. Why? I guess I didn't feel I was that good, or that it was something I could have for just me, that Tory and the rest of the world could not take away from me.

I talked for what seemed like forever with Raph. Telling him when I first started to love art because of books. How I couldn't get enough on the history of art. I shared all of my favorite artists; Warhol, Pollock, Frankenthaler, Picasso, Van Gogh. I told him how I painted with my grandmother Eve. Yes, the evil mother of my mother actually loved to paint and loved to have me around.

My grandmother Eve, I could never figure that one out...

Why she was so fucking mean to my mother and not to me. It was as though she forgot I was Tory's child. She would talk in French and English, mixing the languages to make sure I knew a little of both while explaining The Impressionists. Eve would also talk about what it was like for her as a younger woman with a twinkle in her eye. Oh the stories she would tell of her dancing on tables in small speakeasy's in NYC and the romance of the city. I loved to hear about all of it. We bonded deeply over the paint.

We were in a groove, so comfortable together, but my phone interrupted us. It was Dominique. I was quickly brought back to reality. Excusing myself, practically running to the ladies room, I answered the phone in sheer panic. I tried to slow my role with deep breaths before saying anything, but I was out of breath.

"Angel, I apologize for leaving without my phone. I am back on the boat now; I will come over to pick you up after a quick change of clothes... Say half an hour, ok?" Dominique apologized.

"Yes, yes, that sounds good." My voice cracked.

"You sound strange Allie, are you ok... Are you angry with me?" Concerned, he questioned me.

"No, no I could never be mad at you." Dismissing the notion, I laughed as I regained my composure. I was thankful that he wasn't standing before me. He would have known I was lying.

"Aw, good, I will see you soon. Can you come to the front of the hotel angel?" Sweetly he requested.

"Yes, of course." I was so relieved that he wasn't coming in, also that I had a few more minutes with Raph.

Not knowing a lot about Raph, but wow, I knew this. I really liked this man. He made me feel at ease, like an equal. Plus, he was so funny, kind, hot, young, naughty, and super smart. I didn't know it then, but this wasn't the last evening I would spend with him. Raph would be in my life at some point. When I needed him most, he would appear. When would be the next time?

"I'm sorry, but I have to leave after this drink. I have dinner." Returning to my seat, I grabbed for the bill.

"Hey, I will take care of your check. Allie, can I call you in two weeks when I'm back in New York?" Touching my hand underneath the table.

"I don't know, I think that's wrong, you know who I'm with. I don't think it is possible to be friends. He would never approve of this." Carefully explaining with great remorse. "Besides, why do you want to be my friend?!" I joked.

"Are you kidding me, Allie? You are funny, beautiful, and a smart ass. Why wouldn't I want to know you?!" Raph brushed my chin with his fingers. I couldn't hold back my flirty laughter; he was so sweet. He and Dominique were polar opposites, and I felt drawn to him because of it.

"If we ever see one another in Manhattan, then it will be a sign that we are meant to be friends, fair enough?" I half-smiled.

"Sure. What am I supposed to say, Allie? You're the boss." Kissing my hand, I didn't resist. I was drawn to him, and I think he knew this; I know he did.

"I have to go now, sorry, I hope to see you in the Big Apple, thanks for the drinks!" Walking away, I smiled, shaking my head. I couldn't hold the happiness in.

"You will, Allie baby," calling behind me.

"Raph…" Turning back to the table with a grin.

"Allie?" He questioned.

"Keep this between us, this drink, ok?" Pleading to his serious side.

"Yes, of course, sweetheart, I get it." Raph understood the magnitude of Dominique's need to possess me. He had witnessed it first-hand. I believed him; I don't think he would intentionally hurt me, ever. He might even possibly end up my savor someday.

I left thinking how serendipitous that was, and then my butterflies soon turned to nerves. What was I doing? Sitting with Raph, betraying my boyfriend? Dominique would have lost his mind seeing me blush and flirt with another man, especially him. What, am I crazy? I sat with him for over an hour drinking Champagne in a romantic corner. I needed to forget Raph and focus on Dominique. He was my everything. How could I forget him so easily? Am I turning into Tory?

I walked out of the lobby, and sitting outside proudly in a Red Pista Ferrari was Dominique. He quickly jumped from the driver's seat when he saw me.

"Wow, angel, you look stunning!" Shaking his head, smiling so proudly at me. Just minutes before, I was giving my attention to his nemesis. "My lady," he opened my door to the flashy sports car.

"Hello stranger, I missed you!" Grabbing him softly before he helped me into the passenger seat. Dominique running back to his side, was downright ecstatic to see me. "Now angel, I will take you to one of my favorite restaurants for some of the best Barolo red wine and steak!" He looked at me with such admiration, kissing my hand, pulled me into him for a kiss on the lips.

"I love you." Tilting my head with a cute smile. I looked into his beautiful blue eyes and was right back loving him more than the entire world.

"Allie...I love you so much... you have no idea," he confessed repeatedly. I know he meant it; I could see it all over his gorgeous face. We were off for our date night. The only thing on my mind now and tonight was going to be him.

We made our way to Fontvieille, which was still considered Monaco, but was on the other side of a mountainous rock where the royal castle sat. We had to drive under it through a winding tunnel to get to the other side. The drive opened to a small port that was lined with posh restaurants. Fontvieille was quaint but vibrant.

Pulling up to his favorite spot, a modern restaurant glowing with gold lights called Beefbar. The street was lined with top-notch establishments side by side, one after the next. A buzzy place full of sexy people that were impeccably dressed. The interior had low lighting, tables, and dark blues and browns; it was masculine yet beautiful and inviting. Walking in, the smells were mouthwatering. It didn't surprise me when the owner greeted us at the door.

"Ciao Dominique, come stai amico mio?" The thirty-something, attractive man greeted him warmly, asking him how he was doing. Polished, elegant, all in black from head to toe, except for a very defined Richard Mille gold watch. He had thick silver, short hair, and clear blue eyes.

"Amico Riccardo, sono fantastico. Che ne dici di te, che cosa hai fatto?" Dominique said hello and asked Riccardo how he was doing.

"My girlfriend, Allie." Dominique proudly pulled me in on their conversation. I didn't know Italian, but I could tell by the hug that they had known one another for a long time. "Of course, she is. You are stunning. It is a pleasure to meet you. I've been telling Dominique for years to find a lady to marry." Riccardo teased.

"I don't think she'll marry me; she's too good for me!" Dominique squeezed my hand.

"I don't know, you are a pretty decent guy.... But for real, Allie, he's fantastic." Winking, Riccardo kissed my cheek, welcoming me like family. "Let me show you to your seats, my friend, and promise we'll have lunch before you leave." Riccardo insisted, guiding us to a beautiful table in the middle of the windows and the center of the room. I could get used to this; I am getting used to this.

Everyone in the place paid close attention to us. It is not every day Riccardo came out to greet people at his restaurant; it caused a bit of chatter around us. Loving the attention from the crowd, but also that of my lover, introduced again as his girlfriend. I think he was impressed with how I looked on his side.

"Thank you, Riccardo, and yes, let's get together. I'll call you tomorrow. Can you come to the boat?" Dominique asked, kissing his friend as a gesture, the European way.

"Yes, I would love to. I'll bring some nice wines. God knows, you don't have any," Riccardo joked, leaning in to kiss my hand, quickly following up with my chair. He was such a good soul. I loved the energy he brought to the place, pure star quality, feeling honored to have met him, such a close friend of Dominiques. This meant a lot in guy code, sharing a love interest, that is.

Dominique ordered us Champagne to start and then asked the waiter to decant one of his bottles of wine. One of "his" bottles of wine, I thought. What does he have, his own collection? This is intriguing; who does he not know, and what does this man not have? "As I told you, my angel, this restaurant's known for their steaks. Riccardo and his family are the biggest beef importers in Europe. They have many restaurants, this being the first and in my opinion the best." Dominique spoke intently about the exquisite place and his friend. I listened closely. I was like a sponge and wanted to know more, anything more, anything he had to say.

We had a romantic evening filled with big red Italian wines, a super Tuscan, and a Barolo. Dominique feasted on a porterhouse, and I a filet mignon. Meeting someone close to him felt significant, I knew that he was in awe of me. He told me about some of his favorite spots in Italy and promised to take me. I was impacting his heart; he had already captured mine from day one.

We said our goodbyes and headed towards the exit when a petite woman stopped us on the way out. She had long gray hair, small attractive framed eyeglasses, and spoke English to him. My guess is she was a bit older than Dominique.

"Hello Dominique, long time no see!" She said with a glare, ignoring me altogether. "Dominique, I've been calling you all day. I know when you are in Monaco, this is my home, and I have ears everywhere!" She got a bit louder.

"Jolie, I will have to reach out tomorrow", as he grabbed my hand, walking around her. Dominique was cold when he left. She knew better than to follow us because she stayed in the restaurant. Our car was waiting for us when we shuffled out.

"Who was that?" I asked.

"Allie, I don't want that woman to ruin our perfect night... Please angel ... I will explain it to you in the morning. Can you agree with that?" Firmly, yet politely he asked.

"Yes, of course, let's not let her spoil anything." I smiled, kissing his hand in the car.

"Did I tell you that you looked stunning this evening, angel?" Smiling with his devilish grin. I couldn't help but melt.

"Yes, love you did," gushing from happiness nibbling away on his finger.

"You keep that up, and we won't make it out to listen to music," Dominique joked, but his eyes were intense as he watched me suck on his finger. "Allie, I mean it. I'm getting hard. Stop, young lady." Pulling his hands slowly away from my mouth onto the steering wheel.

"Yes, sir... I'll be good. Where are we going? You said music!" Shrieking like a kid with ice cream.

"I'm taking you to a famous lounge, a live music venue called Sass Café. Sass is a friend, and so is his son Sammy." Dominique described the place and the action it held inside. "It's a hot spot in town, always starts the night with live music, and it's not too big, so you don't get lost in it. I have a table next to the piano, I promise it'll be a shit show, but a fun one to watch."

"I'm excited. I haven't been to a music club before!" All these firsts were just grooming me to quickly become an adult, not just an adult but a powerful woman.

"I will show you the world Allie, my little angel." Dominique was sweet with me; I think he really was in love. He also enjoyed all of the new experiences I had with him, in and out of the bedroom.

We drove back to the other side of the palace; Monte-Carlo. Dominique explained to me this was the heart of Monaco, the bustling, more flamboyant side. How exciting, I thought. Dominique promised me we would take a tour tomorrow on his motorcycle; it was a better way to see it with less traffic. He explained that motorcycles didn't have the rules we had in the U.S. They could readily pass and didn't have to stay in traffic. This seemed really exhilarating, and so did the night ahead of us.

On our way to Sass Café, we passed the Monte-Carlo Casino, the hotel, and Café de Paris. I was amazed by the beautiful structure of the buildings that were built in the 1800s. They were jumping out of the pages of history and fairytales. My eyes didn't know what to look at first; the exotic cars that lined the roundabout at the casino? All of the glamorous people walking around? I was so intrigued by the fashion here, I lived in NYC since I was twelve years old, but this was taking it to another level. I had never seen so many women dripping in diamonds, and I mean diamonds, so big that they couldn't be real, could they? All of the men had significant looking watches. Some appeared to be made out of solid gold. I would not have said gaudy, but instead flashy, if anything. The rumors were correct. This is the Playground of the Rich & Famous! Me Allie Hart here with this man, life could not be any better than this, I'm living in a movie starring myself.

We pulled up to Sass Café, where the valet scattered around the car to open our doors and make their money. A friendly, middle-aged, bald man with glasses quickly took notice and pulled us through the swarms of people in the outdoor area. Crowds of good-looking people were standing with drinks. The alfresco tables on the sidewalk were covered with a red tenting. It looked like something out of Lawrence of Arabia. Hookahs, cigars, cigarettes, cocktails, and Champagne at every table. The sexy young women sat lining the windows, prowling for their kill... wow, it was such a scene. I later found out the girls in the window were high-end prostitutes.

We were taken directly to our table, where there was a bottle of bubbly chilling. Next to the Champagne was our bodyguard. I guess he had driven ahead to meet us upon our arrival. Dominique seemed fine with the crowd, but he didn't want too many people collecting in front or near us. The staff, including the famous Sass, the owner, came by to say hello and introduce himself to me as a sign of respect to my man. It was the first time I had seen Dominique dance; I was impressed by how sexy, and at ease he was. I noticed that he was staring at me the entire time, not even a glance at another woman, and believe me, I thought the ladies were stunning. Looking back, I was just young; in actuality, I really was a showstopper, and he knew it. After all, he made me, partially. We enjoyed the drinks, people, and a few songs, then decided to retire to L'Hermitage. Dominique had arranged that we stay in town to sightsee the next day and arrange massages at the spa.

Entering the hotel, we walked down the extremely long hall filled with French baroque mirrors to our elevator. Our suite overlooked the sea. It was exquisite. White Victorian furniture, high ceilings with antique chandeliers of that period. The four-poster bed was lush, dressed with white, crisp Egyptian cotton sheets and the softest down pillows, sophisticated and alluring.

"Do you like it, angel?" Waiting patiently for my answer.

"I absolutely love it." He made me so happy. Kissing him was all I could think about when he asked me.

I was only a couple of inches beneath him now with these extremely high heels, it felt good not having to reach for my lover's lips, but he thought otherwise.

"Allie, can you go to the bathroom and take everything off for me, including that makeup?" He had hunger in his eyes.

"Yes," I said shyly and left to do as my lover requested.

Dominique had turned the lights down and lit a few candles, taken off his clothes, and was lying naked on the bed. He looked like an Adonis, so proud and gorgeous with his tan body in the low-lit room. I stripped down, feeling sexy as I walked over to him. He made me feel sensual and pretty without makeup, shoes, hair... anything. I felt completely loved for the first time, and all I wanted to do was please him in any way I could. I was his to have.

"I love your body.... come here," pulling me on top to straddle him while he stared deep into my eyes. "You are mine... you know that, right?" His eyes filled up with water. Dominique was feeling a lot of emotion. I could visibly see his vulnerability for the first time. "I am yours... I am, forever... I don't see anything but you in my life. You have me." Staring back into his gaze, allowing me to see him, was a bonding experience. I think back on that feeling, and I get weak. I long for this again. My innocence was my ally. My experiences have become my enemy.

Grabbing me by the waist, placing my private parts upon his face. Licking and sucking me, moving his mouth in all directions until he read what my body was telling him. He wouldn't let up.... moving on his face until I surrendered to his thirst and screamed his name.

"I love you... I ... I love you, Dominique! I'm cumming for you!" He slowly released me and smiled as I slid away.

"I love you too angel... remember what I said, you are mine, and no one can have this, except for me." He laid me on my back, entering me with a total thrust, pushing into me over and over fast and hard as he filled me up with his hot liquid. "You are mine!" Crying out, fully immersed in his orgasm. I loved feeling him deep inside. A bond was getting undeniably more potent every day that we were together.

We were completely done, exhausted from the evening.

"Let's get some rest. I will show you Monaco tomorrow." Tucking me into his arm. "Goodnight... I love you."

I don't remember anything after those words. I was utterly content. Loving this man put my young mind at ease.

I woke alone; Dominique was not in bed. Glancing over at

the clock, it said 10:30 am. Wow, I must have been tired. I slept nine hours. I got up and showered, fixed my hair in a slicked-back ponytail, added a light coat of mascara and a touch of bronzer. I didn't really like a lot of makeup, still don't to this day. Dominique would say that I was beautiful with or without, so I felt daytime was a better choice for "no makeup, makeup." That is what Tory used to call it when you applied some, just enough to make you look fresh.

Elegance was still in order, so I chose a long white flowing dress, pairing it with a flat, tan, Hermes mule. I wore my diamond earrings and a silver, Daytona Rolex watch, which was sophisticated and fulfilling. The only missing thing was my Dominique. I tried reaching him on his phone, but no answer. Deciding on a tea, I texted him. "Hi my love, where are you? I'm going to get my caffeine fix. Let me know if I should come to you. XO." I went to the lovely café, on the outdoor terrace, under an umbrella. I waited and waited... still I hadn't heard from him. After forty minutes, I got the check and took a stroll to see what the spa looked like. I texted him once again, letting him know, but again nothing.

It was confusing as I had to take two elevators to get to the spa. I must have taken a wrong turn because I ended up at the other end of the hotel, in yet another lobby. This place was a palace in itself, just going on and on in all directions. I asked yet another concierge station for directions, and they pointed me on my way to another set of elevators. I must have missed walking through the hotel. I jumped into the lift and hit "spa." I was thrilled I had finally found my way and was going to see the world-class facility. Little did I know who would be right in front of me once again.

The door opened, and there he was, my heart fell to the ground... Raph! He too, looked like he had seen a ghost.

"Allie! Wow... I'm sorry you surprised me, hence the look I'm giving you now!" Shaking his head with confusion and a welcoming smile.

"Yes.... wow is right, you seem to be everywhere that I am, mister!" I was secretly flipping out inside. This guy could light up a room; he was so charismatic.

"How are you?" Reaching over to touch my hand. I didn't pull back initially. It felt nice, but I didn't want to be seen like this with another guy other than Dominique, so I slowly moved my hand away from his.

"I'm terrific...... just checking out the spa." Smiling, I pointed in the direction of the receptionist, where I should have been going if I had known better.

"Yeah, ok... it's a....really fabulous.... you, um.... you'll love it." Mumbling as he looked me over. I wanted to burst into laughter. Why was he acting like this? Do I now make him uneasy? The conversation was kind of sweet, but still, you could cut the nervous energy with a knife. I like this man a lot! How could I belong to someone else and still feel like this every time I see him? Raph felt the connection, and he didn't seem to care about Dominique's claims, but I did as the nagging fear came knocking.

We engaged in small talk about Monaco and his plans for the day. I didn't have much to contribute since I was new to this place. Laughing at his silly jokes, we naturally wandered into the spa gift shop to have more privacy. We weren't there for more than five minutes when I heard Dominique's voice in the room.

"Allie?" Dominique spoke without any type of warmth in his tone.

"Hello! I've.... been looking for you!" Announcing while hugging him. Dominique didn't acknowledge my words. Placing one arm around me, he quickly turned to Raph.

"You again, I asked you like a gentleman to stay away from Allie, you started shit with me, and now here you are again!" He stepped closer to Raph.

"You should let Allie decide who she wants to be friends with... Man, are you that insecure?" Raph barked back in his cocky and predictable manner. Raph was fearless and his own person for such a young man. He wasn't intimidated by anything. I admired his strength, but still, I hated the conflict.

"You want to play with me, boy?" Puffing his chest towards Raph. "Allie, can you tell this joker you do not want to be friends with him?" Dominique clearly wasn't asking.

I paused briefly and realized my back was up against the wall. I could not betray Dominique. He was my friend, my first boyfriend, my lover, my everything. If he left me, I would be nothing again.

"Raph, this is my choice. I choose to not cause pain or friction here; I have to respect Dominique's wishes. We cannot be friends... Please, don't do this anymore. I can't." Declaring my loyalty, I grabbed Dominique's arm in a way to let him know I belonged to him and only him.

"Allie, when you grow apart, which you will, I'll be around. You will know how to find me." Looking at only me with great sadness in his beautiful, green eyes but swiftly changed his tone as he turned to Dominique. "You, good fucking luck holding onto her... She will find this shit tedious and dump your French ass. Girls like Allie are independent, stronger than you give her credit for!" He left kicking over a rack. I felt shitty. I flirted with Raph and then, in one second, destroyed him. Will he ever forgive me? What kind of person does that? A terrible one, but what choice did I really have?

"Thank you for backing me, Allie." Dominique kissed my forehead in what almost appeared to be relief.

"I love you. You know that. Don't be jealous of him. He just loves to get under your skin, and you let him... why?" I asked.

"I don't know, Allie! I don't fucking get it. I never felt like this before. I've never wanted to rip someone's head off like that. I guess what it comes down to is that he lives in New York City, and so do you...I don't like it ... I just don't fucking like it... alright!" Grabbing my waist, pulling me in for a more demanding than usual kiss on the mouth.

"Ouch, you cut my lip." I could taste blood in my mouth.

"I'm... sorry... I don't know what that was. You don't deserve that." Rummaging through his pockets, he found a tissue and patted my lip. Dominique was jealous, beyond his own comfort zone. I didn't like this side of him, but I was in some sort of way responsible for all of it. I didn't realize it then, but I do now. Playing men like Tory would become second nature in my life.

I changed the conversation to relax us at the spa. Dominique had made some romantic plans for us, first a couple's massage and then two pedicures. He liked being pampered as much as I did. Afterward, we got on a motorcycle for a romantic ride to see the beauty of the landscape. I held my arms tightly around him. Sightseeing around the small country was breathtaking. We drove along the narrow streets filled with shops and cafes, also taking in the scenery by foot along the sea wall, where the locals would swim. We seemed to have put the entire Raph thing behind us. It was just two lovers in an old romantic Grace Kelly movie.

At the end of the day, we returned to our suite. Dominique appeared to be seemingly upset while pouring his Scotch.

"Allie, please, can you join me? Requesting me by his side.

"Yes." Replying with zero hesitation as I sat next to him.

"Can I trust you? This Raph character has been around more times than I am comfortable with."

Waiting patiently for my response. My heart stopped, my face began to burn, I felt guilty. Flirting and having feelings for

Raph were over. All that was left was me, "insecure Allie," the little girl in the shadow of her mother. Is he going to leave me? What did I do? I couldn't hold it; I was physically sick. I ran to the master bathroom, slamming the door with my foot, barely making it to the toilet when everything from lunch came hurling out of me.

I heard Dominique knocking, but I could not answer between takes. Asking if I were ok, offering to grab me a bitters and club soda, I could hear him walk away from the door. I stood up slowly. As I walked out of the stall, my head was spinning, gripping the double sinks. I washed my face with cold water, which eased my spins, and brushed my teeth. Sweaty and as white as a ghost, I looked like a frightened infant, so young and frail once again. It pulled me back into my terrified feelings of losing my mother. I was always afraid of her leaving me. I couldn't go back to the old Allie, alone and scared. I took several deep breaths and calmed my weary soul. "Pull it together, Pull it together, Allie!" Slapping my face for some gumption.

I heard his footsteps once again approaching the door. "Allie, can I come in?" Pleading for me to open the door. "Yes...come in." Speaking in a small voice.

"Angel, are you alright? What's wrong......did you eat something bad? Was it me? Talk to me, please... I'm concerned." Remorsefully, grabbing my limp hand.

"I... I um... do you want me to be honest with you?" Raising my voice slightly.

"Yes, please." Patiently he waited to hear what I had to say as he sat on the tub with his hands at his sides. I paused for about ten seconds while I searched for the words to say, "I'm scared... I'm scared I'm going to lose you every time you get upset with me... it just gives me a panic attack......I love you so much that it hurts me, physically hurts me! If I lose you... I just, I can't... I can't, Dominique!" Bellowing out to him.

"Allie, calm down. That isn't going to happen! I'm such a jerk for doing this to you!" Wrapping his strong arms around my slump body. He picked me up, carried me into our bed, laid me on my stomach, and began to caress my back to relax me. "Now now...don't cry, angel. I love you. Nothing bad is ever going to happen to us. We are together. I am yours, and you are mine." Repeating the words softly in my ear. I was exhausted from the stress of it all and fell asleep.

I woke to Dominique sitting next to me on the bed. Happy to see him, I sat up slowly, landing in his arms.

"Hi, beauty. You seem rested. Are you okay now?" Holding me close to him.

"Yes, my love, I'm sorry that I overreacted," I smiled, looking down.

"No, I'm the one that is sorry... you shouldn't be apologizing. I made you feel that way. I won't do it again." Pushing me slowly away, he presented a small black box. "I have something for you, angel." Placing it in my hands.

"For me?" I asked with a goofy smile.

"Yes, silly for you... you're the only love of my life." Handing me the box. I opened it. It was a watch shaped like a serpent by Bulgari, to my surprise. He called it the Serpenti Tubogas. The double spiral watch that appeared to be pink gold was actually 18-carat rose gold. It was like nothing I had ever seen in my life or in magazines. The face was full of many small diamonds. It sparkled like a star in the sky and wrapped around my wrist twice, not once but twice!

"I don't know what to say... Thank you, my love. I don't deserve this." Falling into his arms, I knew he had forgiven me. I think at this point, I was the one giving forgiveness. He loved that gifts were for me unexpected and that I was utterly, completely grateful. I think it made him want to give more.

Dominique never wanted me to see him as anything but kind. If I did, I think it would have broken his heart. He loved me, his gifts were another way to show me, but he knew I would not have cared as long as he never stopped loving me, ever.

"How can I ever thank you for everything you brought me, Allie. You are my sweet Allie. I will make sure you are always safe; I know you want that......It's almost time to go back to New York, and I've come up with a plan... I would like to talk about it later, ok." Placing his hands on my face, he kissed me passionately. I was so crazy about this man, and my thoughts swiftly moved to pleasing him.

"Yes, my love, later we can talk, but now I feel like doing

something else with you." Pulling my top off with confidence, climbing towards him on the bed. We made love for hours, kissing and sucking. I found my rhythm with him. He could see how I developed into a butterfly right before his eyes. Sex solved the jealousy or made it better. I think it still does. Doesn't it?

Famished afterwards, we snacked on fruit as we got ready to head out for our last evening on the town. I ran a bath as I picked through my clothes in the enormous closet I had to myself. I wanted to wear something bright and fun to go with my blingy watch and ring. I decided on a short, green Hermes dress featuring strappy cut-out features on the top. It was the same green as my eyes, so it really made them pop. I wore rose gold pumps to match my accessories and asked the spa earlier to send someone up to help with my hair. I wanted those "beach waves" I had grown fond of. They obliged, and Dominique laughed as he brought the young lady in from the salon.

"You got this down now, don't you, angel." Grinning, he showed the girl into my bathroom.

"I have to look good for you, don't I?" I smirked, closing the doors to the master bathroom. I turned on some light lounge music and poured a glass of wine from a bucket Dominique had sent in for me. I was always in the forefront of his mind, which made me smile. The little romantic gestures almost meant more to me then.

The girl from the salon did a fantastic job from head to toe.

My smoky eyes and light lipstick were flawless. My skin was dewy and shimmery gold from my body bronzer. She even bronzed my legs, arms, chest, breasts, and even my feet with what she called "liquid gold." I had never heard of such a thing, but wow, I thought this looked radiant. My skin was glowing like JLo in a video or her on the cover of a magazine. I walked confidently out to the living space of the suite. Dominique eagerly stood up to greet me. "Magnificent! Très belle. Je t'aime mon coeur." Walking over, picking me up, he spun me around. "You look stunning. I'm speechless, Allie.... you're a model....so fucking hot angel," growling in delight. *I was hot... me hot? This man loved me, and I thought I was hot!* I felt confident, older, and ready to be on his arm for the night. I could not have felt more alive! As if I could not have been more thrilled, my sexy man was in an all white, shawl collar tuxedo by Tom Ford. He was so gorgeous; he literally took my breath away. I later discovered his tux was actually straight off the runway at Tom Ford's latest show. In the coming months, I would get to meet Tom with Dominique and eventually walk the catwalk for him. That was the beginning of my infatuation with Tom Ford and his clothes.

Entering the lobby, workers in the hotel dropped what they were doing to see us out, as the other hotel guests stared at us. We were a power couple, or at least we appeared to be such; gorgeous, rich, tall, and in love.

"Angel, do you like Peruvian food?" Opening the door of a black Phantom Rolls Royce. "I've never had it. A lot of firsts for me... Nice car, by the way," replying as he guided my bottom into the backseat and with the other hand, assisted me to a sitting position. Such a gentleman, always made sure he took care of me in every way. Fuck I am so lucky.

CHAPTER 15

Coya oh Boya

I thought it was strange that we pulled down a long road cutting through the private residential gate. Oddly enough, there were signs for the restaurant, alongside an advertisement for Jimmy'z nightclub. We drove into the very posh neighborhood ending in a big circular drive. I asked him why they would have a restaurant here, and he explained, it's Monaco, everything is exclusive. The cars were lined up to make their grand entrance at the restaurant. It reminded me of something you would see on a red carpet event in Hollywood; lights, press, gorgeous people. Pulling up, there was a familiar face again, the bodyguard. Why did my boyfriend have this bodyguard? Were we in harm's way? I would later in life discover a lot more about my perfect Dominique, probably more than I should have. I couldn't wait to jump out of the car with my divine love, and he couldn't either.

"I love you, angel. You look spectacular. I couldn't be prouder, having you on my arm, as my girl." Kissing my hands softly and then my neck.

"Please, that is my spot. It drives me crazy!" Wiggling away from his nibble, I was jumping out of my skin; we were next to arrive for the masses! The driver opened Dominique's door, and then the bodyguard opened mine. He swiftly walked around the car to meet me, never allowing me to walk without his hand or arm. It was a sign to me that he not only had class but that he also wanted to show me off. I wasn't the little girl he told "not to touch him in public" I looked like a 21-year-old, and not just a twenty-something, but a sexy and sophisticated young woman that stood out.

Entering the low-lit restaurant, it felt more like a lounge than a place to eat. The music was fueled by a young, hot, Latino DJ. The extensive bar took over the left side, filled with exceptional looking people enjoying artful cocktails. On the right side, a busy open kitchen overlooking a massive dining room. Leaving the main cafe and bar that led to a substantial yet exclusive terrace, I assumed it was the best because it overlooked the Mediterranean. Not only were there heart-stopping views outside, but such a scene on the inside, resembling a jungle and everyone ready to mate. Coya was considered the hippest restaurant "currently" in town, so it was a no-brainer for our last evening in Monte-Carlo.

We were greeted by a model-like, tall blonde named Isabella. She knew Dominique and greeted him by name. I thought that was admirable; she's really good at her job. Isabella had a lovely way about her, offering a big smile and a hello to me, which I thought was extremely important.

"I have your table ready. Please follow me," Isabella led us to our nest for the evening. Wow, I thought to myself, this place is on fire. I could see what all the fuss was about. Dominique thanked Isabella for seating us immediately and handed her a 500 Euro bill. My guess is Isabella remembers currency, not just people...

"Why not?" I thought, "girl's gotta eat."

I loved the attention, walking past the onlookers while they waited for their tables. It was something I was beginning to get used to. We sat in the center of the dining terrace. It was perfect, we had first row seats to the whole place, and everyone could wonder who we were. Dominique requested the wine list and handed me the cocktail menu.

"Allie, do you want to start with a drink first? We can have wine with dinner angel. They are known for their mixologist." He smiled, looking up to tell me about them. "Damn, I forgot the rest of what I was about to say. You are very distracting this evening. Allie, I'm getting fucking hard just looking at you." Grabbing my hand, pushing it against his stiff cock. Damn.... he is spectacular, so fucking sexy. I felt warm from just knowing he was hard for me.

"I want to kiss you there." Rubbing it, I licked my lips, teasing him.

"Stop that, young lady." Dominique took my hand in his.

"Love, can you help me with a drink? I'm not sure what I would like." I asked.

"Of course, angel." He leaned over to explain in the loud restaurant. Telling me about the liquors to educate me on how they would taste. He knew I didn't like anything that tasted like alcohol, so I decided on a pisco sour after a brief moment. The cocktail was delicious, and so was the energy of the place. Latin music filled the room as the crowd began to dance at the bar.

A very handsome, charismatic mid-thirties man with blonde

hair, dark seductive eyes, a sculpted face and a muscular, yet lean 6'1" tattooed frame appeared in front of our table.

"Hey, Dominique... I thought that was you!" Smiling as they shook hands and stood to hug him as well.

"James, it's been a while. How are you?" Dominique was happy to see him. "Angel, this is a good friend of mine, James John. This man is a world-class designer." Guiding me to my feet to introduce me to James.

"You are stunning!" James looked me over as I rose.

"Hey now...hands off!" Dominique laughed, tucking his hands around my waist. "This is my Allie." Introducing me as his.

"Hello, Allie, a pleasure to meet you." James eagerly kissed my cheeks, still looking me over.

"Thank you, it's a pleasure to make your acquaintance. I know your clothes very well... Who doesn't, right?" Attempting to flatter one of the most prominent designers in the world.

"I insist you bring this lady into my store tomorrow at The Metropole... Allie would rock my clothes!" James said loudly to be heard over the DJ.

"Let's meet over there tomorrow around 11 am, and you can dress her." Winking, Dominique acted as if he had already set it up beforehand. I'm not sure if he did or didn't to this day.

"I would very much like that, and yes, I will be there, but

116

only because of Allie." James hugged Dominique as they said their goodbyes. Bowing to me, wearing a wicked smile as he left. Naughty naughty, you could tell, but also full of great energy, it was bursting from his pores.

Minutes after James left, we received a bottle of Champagne.

"Compliments of Mr. John." Our waiter presented us with a bottle of Cristal Champagne. "Thank him for me, please." We insisted.

Dominique ordered many dishes of Peruvian food for me to try. The flavors popped; it fit the place. Dining on roasted sea bass, tuna tataki, prawns, and squid perfectly paired up with Dominique's wine choices. It was a lively place that soon after became a dance club. James had tons of Champagne bottles sent to his table with loads of sparklers lit up. It was quite a scene. He seemed to love entertaining his group and all of the others in the restaurant. A natural showman, Dominique called him.

"Hey, little angel," Dominique whispered in my ear. "You look so fucking good, Allie; I can't wait to lick you from head to toe." Tickling my ear while kissing it lightly. I felt so fortunate, taking his hand and putting it on my chest directly over my heart.

"You make it race every time you touch me." Leaning in as I kissed his full lips.

"I love you, Allie, I really do. I just... wow.... You really know how to get to me." Dominique turned, kissing me briefly. I don't think he was much for PDA, but he really lost himself when it came to me. "Let's go say goodbye to James." Requesting, we paid our check and walked over to his table. Dominique leaned in to talk to him. It was deafening at this point, so they struggled with communication. James' table must have had at least twenty people.

One, in particular, caught my eye, a stunning brunette. Smiling as she grabbed me for a hug, she spoke in my ear, telling me it was nice to meet you. I was surprised at how much makeup and lip injections she had for such a young woman. I didn't feel I needed it, my lips were naturally full, but I was still pretty amazed that she wasn't alone at the table. It appeared that all of the girls she sat with overdid their lips, boobs, and butts too! I was thin, tall, had only b cups, and I never thought to even put anything in my chest. For me, it looked painful and odd. James asked us to join him at Jimmy'z, but Dominique declined his offer nicely, telling James we had to go, that we were tired. Laughing, James said, "I bet you are." Once again turned to me, "Allie, can't wait to see you tomorrow.... make sure he doesn't cancel on me, ok?!" He joked, and I agreed to hold him to it.

"One second!" James shouted, while pulling his girlfriend close to him. "Let's get a photograph before you leave."

"Ok, sounds good." Dominique agreed."

"I'll send it to you, man." James loved the camera. He was plastered all over social media. I assumed we would be too in less than five minutes. I was freaking out; this is an incredible thing.

We said our goodbyes, jumping into a blacked-out Range

Rover.

"I had them bring another car, so they could grab our things from the hotel and bring them back to the boat, angel." Opening my door, but first pulling me one last time to steal a kiss, then pushing my bottom up to assist with my high heels.

"That was an incredible night, thank you," nuzzling into his body. I even loved the smell of his armpits. How strange of me, I thought. Dominique liked where I was in his arms and slowly put his other hand on my thigh. I immediately had a strong reaction; he could hear me gasp lightly. That made him want to go further up my dress, he did, lightly brushing the outside of my panties. I felt myself getting turned on by his light caresses. "You're a little wet, aren't you?" He teased, rubbing me ever so slightly, harder. My anticipation was growing. I couldn't hold back from touching him through his pants. The play was getting heated as we pulled up to the yacht.

Pulling me along quickly to our bedroom. "I want you so fucking bad...please.... come here, angel." Dominique held me while we lay kissing passionately for a while. I insisted on taking my dress off. It was getting in the way. Wanting to make my lover even crazier, I headed for my closet and found a little number that would do the trick. I put on a cream colored corset with small lacy bottoms to match. I added some volume to my hair by flipping it upside down, walking back into our room. Dominique was laying on some pillows in just his pants. He looked like a god, so strong and virile. I could see that he was turned on. It was always a giveaway.

"Why do you have pants on?" I teased.

"You look like a cat looking for its prey, you naughty girl." Dominique, pulling me on top of him.

"Not so fast. I need to take these off you," I ordered, tugging at his buckle.

"Angel, oh how you have blossomed." Allowing me to work his pants off, now exposing his hard, glistening cock. He flipped me on my back. "Let me look at you... wow, Allie.... how did I get so lucky?" He smiled at me so lovingly. It was as though he had waited for me to come into his life. "I love you, angel." Kissing me deeply.

"I love you, Dominique," I lightly moaned.

"Can I lick you?" Begging for it, as he brushed his finger against my pulsating privates.

"Please... yes," I whimpered. Making his way across my breasts, kissing the tops that were peeking out of my corset, then to my thighs, back to my sweet spot. Sucking my panties, I could feel his hot tongue through the lace. Teasing me, then pulling them off to expose me fully. Kissing my inner thighs, leading to my wetness, slowly working circles around my pussy, massaging my insides with his fingers. I loved his tender touch; it made my body feel things I never thought possible. I ached...I wanted him inside of me, but he told me I would have to wait for it. Pushing harder on my clit, he had me. I was losing my fucking mind. I felt the buildup and couldn't hold on any longer.

"Sweetheart, I'm going to cum for you, don't stop... don't stop... I'm cumming right now." Releasing all over his beautiful face.

Slowly moving away, he came up to meet me with a kiss. I could taste myself inside of his mouth. I liked it. Gripping his manhood, he slowly pushed his cock deep inside of my wet privates, thrusting over and over. I loved how he filled me up with his large cock. I never knew it could feel like this; I only imagined. I loved this man so very much. I would let him do anything to me, absolutely anything. He was mine, and I was his. Pushing deeper and deeper, over and over, he was wild with excitement. My love was on his threshold.

"Allie... Allie... fuck... It feels so fucking good, angel!" Crying out, he collapsed on me.

We laughed a bit because we were high on our orgasms. Now I understand all of the hype. This is what love is; making love is. I would make love to this man over and over for quite a long time, or at least it seemed like a long time, but like all good things, they came to an end.

At least in this little world we were living in, they did. I still have mind-blowing experiences. If I didn't, I couldn't remember all of this so well, now could I?

I don't remember passing out; I just did. Waking to a smiling face, my man laying next to me.

"Are you watching me sleep?" I giggled.

"As a matter of fact, yes," replying with a quick kiss on my forehead, "I'm famished!" Sitting up, I declared, "me too. Let's get up." Jumping to his feet, heading for the shower. He looked so hot; his ass was so firm, it looked like a well-trained athlete. I remember him walking away. I couldn't help but smile and race after him.

"Can I come with you?"

"Yes, come on in," grabbing my hand, pulling me into the shower and into him.

"Kiss me," pouting like a girl.

"You know you're asking for it if I start to kiss you... I don't think we'll make it to breakfast," he teased.

"Just kiss me!" Jumping to my tiptoes, I leaned into him. Kissing me lightly, soon after became deeper.

"I love you, Allie, you know that, right? I would do anything for you." Pulling me back slightly to look at me.

"I know you would." I tried to kiss him again, but he kept me at bay. Dropping to his knees, he pushed my legs apart, taking his mouth to my pussy. Eating me furiously until I came.

I don't think he was there for more than five minutes. How did I train my body to react so quickly to him? This man knows how to please and steal my heart. Picking me up to straddle him while he was standing, I wrapped my legs around him. He was hard and ready for me, sliding into me, pressing me against the shower wall.

"I love you," I kissed him deeply.

"I love you," moaning loudly, he was on his threshold. Up and down, working my hips until he came inside of me.

Afterward, he cleaned me with body wash, towel-dried, and wrapped me like a child. So, tender, I thought.

I dressed and walked up to the deck to eat with him. He knew by now what my choices would be for breakfast. I really like that.

"I have your avocado toast and tea prepared for you." Proudly, he stated.

"You are too good to me!" Kissing him before sitting down.

"Get used to it," he smiled. I wish all relationships could be like this. Wouldn't women be easier to deal with? It's not a big secret, women, that is.

CHAPTER 16

Be Kind and Be John'd

"You know, young lady, we have to go see James at his store this morning, that is if he went to bed last night." He was serious, his friend had a big party going on last night, and it didn't appear that it was stopping any time soon when we left. I, however, hoped that their friendship was significant enough to get the star out of bed.

"Oh right, I almost forgot. I don't know his clothes that well. I told him I did, but I really didn't. I think he's the designer that makes the bling trainers and skull dresses?" Waiting for him to confirm.

"Yes, that's him. Very blingy angel!" Shaking his head, adding a chuckle of amusement. "You have to fly back to New York in some of his clothes," stating the obvious.

"I have a feeling if I don't, you may lose your friend," teasing him, I wanted to get going. I was overcharged to try on some of his wild clothes.

We finished breakfast, brushed our teeth, and did a quick change.

"What should I wear to the shop?" Holding up some choices.

"Something you can remove comfortably because the first thing he'll do is have you naked modeling his clothes. After all, he sent me ten text messages last night asking me who you modeled for," Dominique divulged.

"Oh, he did, me a model?... Come on!" Laughing and still holding the clothes.

"You really don't know just how stunning you are...do you?" Shaking his head at me in disbelief, pointing to the white outfit.

"If you say so!" Walking away with my clothes, I had a laugh. With the help of my lover, we opted for a Theory; white linen romper, paired with some strappy gladiator sandals. I chose a small silver bracelet with diamonds that my mother had given me years ago. It was delicate. I loved it. It made me think of her, and for a second, I missed her. That quickly ended when I recalled her pushing me later that night after giving me the bracelet. "Anything wrong, angel?" Dominique could see the empty stare I had. I snapped out of it. "Everything is perfect."

The driver let us out at the world-famous "Metropole" shopping mall's lower entrance near his friend's restaurant, Pacific.

"I want to quickly say hello to my George. He owns this place." Opening the door to a lovely space with a baby grand piano. They were not opened yet, but George was inside making calls. He was a short man with thick eyebrows and curly hair. He had a roly-poly look and a friendly smile. George had a Greek accent and was charming to talk with. I enjoyed his candidness; he didn't have any pretentious behavior; he acted like a regular guy. George had a little Maltese dog named Sugar that he was madly in love with.

"Georgie, this is Allie... She's from New York City."
Introducing me promptly. "Allie, this is George. He happens to
love Manhattan; he went to Harvard. After living in New York
with his first wife." Nudging George.

"Yes, this is true. I believe wife number one and four are
from the Big Apple." George enjoyed a good laugh at his
expense. They spoke about business and family for all of ten
minutes, forming a plan for us to visit George again, but in
Paris, where he too had an apartment. "Thank you, Allie, for
bringing this man in. He is a keeper, one of the good ones.
Dominique, you better marry this one, or I will." Professing
his admiration for me made me blush. We said our goodbyes
and promised to keep in touch. This would not be the last time
I would meet this man, but it wouldn't be with Dominique.
We left, heading inside the attached Metropole shopping mall.
This was not a typical suburban mall; this was a shopping
mecca for the mega-rich.

We passed Rolex, Valentino, Burma, Brunello Cucinello,
Billionaire Italian Couture, Fauchon of Paris, to name a few. There
were small, gold escalators to take you up and down the petite
high-end experience. We rounded a corner, and there it was,
"bling central," James John and his cool symbol JJ lining the rock
star, sex goddess attire he had in his windows. I'd never seen so
many crystals on clothing, shoes, or sneakers. It was like
experiencing an entire show in Las Vegas but on clothing!

I was really looking forward to wearing everything. My eyes

were as big as tennis balls. Dominique noticed my reaction to the store.

"Allie, you like this, don't you?" Laughing at his young girlfriend.

"You have no idea; I can't wait to feel it and try it on!" Expressing my overjoy, we walked in at 11:00 on the dot.

There he was ... the designer we had met last night, so proud to be involved in my experience. He really knew how to lay it on thick, but I didn't mind, I was thrilled to have "The James John" dress. Me.... Me Allie Hart! He wasn't only hot but flashy and talented.

"Hello, Allie, happy you two made it in!" Kissing my cheeks, then turning to Dominique. You could see that their friendship was authentic and not forced. There was mutual respect amongst these two leaders.

"James, Allie is more excited about this store than anything I might have shown her so far in Monaco, so you have a super fan ready to explore your shop!" Explaining diligently, as to embarrass me a bit.

"A willing participant, I like, an exciting participant I love!" Grabbing my arm, James directed me to a blonde model that worked in the store. "Christina will show you to your room. I already emailed ahead to fill the dressing lounge with all my choices. The only thing I was not sure of but guessed was your shoe size. I said 39.... what is it?" James waited for my answer like he already knew the answer. "You're spot on, mister!"

Declaring with a smile. I still couldn't believe I was here and that he came in just for me.

The first thing James picked for me to try was a dress. The 70's glam mini was a concentrate of fuchsia pink sequins decorated with lightning bolt graphics, recalling Ziggy Stardust. In addition, the brand's lettering and James' last name "John" in big letters ran down the entire right side. It had a plunging back and a hook fastening the neckband. James was a genius, pairing it with a crystal-covered suede bootie. The boots had metal buckled straps further characterizing them, a zip-up fastening on the side and this fantastic jewel skull skewered in the iron stiletto. I was in awe. Totally blown away by this uber, rock chic look. Something I would have never thought in a million years I would wear. Still, I saw myself in the mirror fitting perfectly into these well-molded clothes. They were more than clothes; they were wearable art and I the blank canvas.

After helping me fit into the first outfit, Christina teased my hair a bit to add volume, added some dark eyeliner to my lid and some fake mink eyelashes to add to the vibe of my new look as a "Rockstar Goddess." Her words, not mine.

"You look amazing, Allie; I think James is going to want you to walk his shows after he sees this," Christina said it like she meant it.

"Thank you so much for that. You are a sweetheart," gushing in disbelief.

Walking out of the dressing room was empowering as I

strutted onto the main floor, where Dominique and James were enjoying a glass of Champagne. They both stood up in awe, not saying anything for at least ten seconds as I spun around, and then there it was.

"Are you kidding me?! This is fabulous, you... She was born to model my clothes!" Jumping around in amazement, James was losing his mind.

"I think you may be right, man!" Dominique putting a paused clap together made me feel special. I couldn't help but light up.

"Christina, take my iPhone; I need photos with Allie. I have to post this to my Instagram!" Boasting, James handed over his iPhone. James John wants a photograph of me on his Instagram! My heart was beating fast, standing by his side, but contained my composure and struck a sexy pose...I most likely had seen it in a magazine or advertisement. He glanced at it afterward. "Allie, you must model for me, I insist, but first try on some more clothes; we can talk later." Scooting me away. Turning back, jumping into Dominique's arms, I couldn't ignore all of what he did for me today. I needed to acknowledge it with a kiss. I would make sure everyone knew that I loved him. Kissing me back, he was pleased. I could see how much that meant to him, especially in front of his friend.

"Angel go, we want to see more on you." Pushing me by my ass, I walked away giggling. James watched us. I could see for a second, he was into it. Maybe he, too, noticed my immaturity and liked it for himself.

I scurried along with Christina back to the vast dressing room.

"I have to see you in one of these! You have an amazing body; you could wear a sack and look good!" Insisting as she held it up to me. Next, she had me in a silk fabric double-breasted coat dress in red with the lettering KISS all over it, paying tribute to Kiss, the 70's rock band. Pairing it with the outrageously cool heel, she called it one of his classic skull stilettos. The iconic skull is quite literally "skewered" on the metal stiletto. I would in the future wear these more times than I could count.

I loved these shoes and all of the rockstar looks they put on me. There was a short romper that looked adorable, more on the simple side of his designs. Christina explained that James himself would be back in a minute. He wanted to give me something that was not out on the market yet. I waited for this wild man to come back, but I wasn't prepared for how quickly.

"Hello there!" James interrupted me half-naked in my undies, feeling quite comfortable. "Hi!" I answered.

"I have not shown this to anyone, but I know this will fit you. I love this design, and I'm only making this as a couture item for my next show," proudly announced as he put it up to me. It was a breathtaking black full-length number. A plunging neckline, draping, and see-through silk chiffon long dress. On the neck and waist were rhinestone decorations. It was divine. It literally took my breath away.

"Please, Allie, try it on for me," beaming like a young boy. "I must see this on you."

"With pleasure, Mr. John!" Teasing him in my underwear, I shook my hips as I spoke his name. The clothes and his relaxed demeanor left me at ease, I had never experienced anything like this in my life or even in my daydreams! That made him smile as he walked out.

Christina returned to me with two glasses of rosé Champagne and said, "Let's make a toast... to you and your new modeling career," handing me a drink and clinking with hers. I was happy with her toast and a bit thrown back.

"No, but thank you for the compliment!" I shyly took another sip.

"Allie, you don't understand what is going on, do you? James will do anything now to have you work for him... I wouldn't be surprised if you lead his next runway show and campaign! He likes your look and you, for that matter. He's probably devising a contract right now with Dominique." Explaining passionately to me.

"Really... you're serious, aren't you? I never considered modeling." I explained.

"Why? Are you blind? You should. James won't let you walk away when he has his mind made up... there isn't a single person that can stop him." Preparing for what was next, I guess. I couldn't imagine this to be accurate, or could it be?

"I guess we will see what he has to say." Smiling, I held up the last outfit. Christina helped me with my last item. "The Dress," the dress no one has ever seen, not even the press... I was putting it on to model for the designer himself, "James John." I was floating on a cloud, living an actual dream, but it wasn't a dream. It was very real. I felt like a warrior in this dress, strong and fierce. I never imagined clothes could make you feel like this, but now I totally understand.

Looking in the mirror at myself, thinking for the first time, I can be anything I want, I am somebody... Pressing my shoulders back, I walked through the doorway, strutting for the first time to my love and James. They were engaged in chatter, but only for seconds. They both stopped when I walked into the room. I silenced two men from speaking for what seemed like an eternity. Jumping to their feet while talking simultaneously to compliment the dress and compliment me.

"This is super, I love my dress, and now I love you." Dancing around me like a kid.

"Allie, angel... you are fantastic, wow." My love, smiling from ear to ear, Dominique could not believe his eyes.

"My clothes were made for this girl. You have to model for me. I won't take no from you!" James demanded of me. I didn't know if he was serious or not.

"I love them. I do feel like they were made for me, James!" Shyly looking down for a second but quickly remembering that I should not. I am happy, and I deserve this, telling myself this was hard to swallow, but I would grow out of that quickly. After all, I am my mother's daughter.

"Angel, this dress was actually made for you." Turning to me, James held my hands out in front of me. What does this mean? Confused, I questioned the designer.

"We spoke a week ago... Dominique asked me to make something special for you, but what I didn't know is that you would be so fucking stunning in it," the designer boasted, clarifying that my boyfriend had this planned already.

"Seriously, you had this made for me, my love?" Walking to Dominique, I put my hands on his manly shoulders, looking deeply into his eyes, probably never this intensely. "I love you more than anything or anyone. You make me so happy. I don't even know what to say." I cried a soft tear of happiness.

"Allie, ... you deserve this and the world. You are such a good girl." Sweetly he wiped my tears away. I turned my happiness to James, running to him with open arms.

"Thank you, James, thank you!"

"You're welcome, Allie... with pleasure." Loving my reaction, the designer hugged me. "Please, put on a John t-shirt dress... I want you to advertise for me. The rest Christina will box up and have sent to the boat." James was a generous man and a great friend to Dominique. He wasn't just a flashy fashion designer, he was a good person, so I thought. I changed; I couldn't help but overhear them discussing something that had to do with me. My name was brought up several times. I was pretty curious to know exactly what they were talking about. We said our goodbyes and exited the store. I had wondered when he would bring up the conversation that he had without me, but for now, I wanted to just relive the entire experience in my head. It was that good.

Only two more nights on the yacht, then fly back to Paris and home to New York City. I needed to know Dominique's plan for us. I wasn't feeling amazing knowing that we were parting in a couple of days. I actually felt sick, my thoughts turning back to Tory and school. My fantastical life was over, the fairy tale is just that, and he would remember I'm just a kid... right? My self-doubt was all-consuming.

Returning to the boat brought some anxiety. I asked Dominique what his plan was. I needed to talk. I wanted to hear what his idea was for us to be together. Was there one? Am I going to be part of his life? Explaining that we were under no circumstances breaking up, but that he needed to first take a shower before we went through it in detail. He left and left me confused. I thought a drink would kill the racing thoughts, so I did a Tory and made myself a Vodka Martini and gulped it down. I was beginning to understand her need for alcohol. It would be part of my life, and it would hurt a lot of it.

My stomach was a massive ball of knots. I had to know if my mother had emailed me, so I checked on my iPhone. My hope was that she was sending me back to New York City alone and that she decided to run off with another random playboy. After all, she worked mainly from a laptop. She could travel anywhere she so desired. My mother had wealth but would never date anyone who did not have money. She would say, "It's just as easy to date rich as it is poor." I guess it will be forever our family motto. Don't judge me too harshly. I don't like that part of me too much either, but it has served me well. Well past the days that you're reading about now. Let's just say, "like mother, like daughter."

I had a message from her assistant Becky. She wrote that Tory would meet me in two days at The Four Seasons in Paris and that we would travel back to New York together on an early morning flight the following day. Becky also explained that Tory requested a special dinner last night to celebrate. I couldn't imagine what we would be celebrating? I was kind of looking forward to our dinner. I wanted to show her just how grown up her little punching bag got, I said kind of. The other half was not looking forward to her seeing me as a woman. She may wonder how and why I had changed. Suspicion was not a good idea, but I was not, not in a million years hiding away anymore. I wanted to be this Allie, not the scared scrawny kid. Maybe she'll be proud of me?

It hurt like a knife in my heart when I thought of Tory. I couldn't figure out how she could be "that" damaged. Am I that damaged? I was getting good at putting my feelings in small boxes and hiding them away from myself. It was too painful to deal with this shit all of the time. I'm flooded with emotion, overwhelmed with "anything" that is possibly feelings. I might have opened one of the boxes and found me. I am a woman that wants to live my life for me, not her anymore. I will be heard; she will listen to me. I'm not going to be afraid anymore, am I?

I was sitting in the dark looking up at all the stars when

Dominique found me. Monaco had a brilliant sky full of them for me to stare at and think. I wondered what was out there, was someone watching me and saying, "what a child she is." My thoughts quickly moved to the beautiful specimen standing before me. He was something of a mystical god like Zeus and I was just a mortal, so fragile and small in the world. If he loved me anything would be possible.

"Angel, what a beautiful night, no?" Sitting down, he reached his strong arms around me.

"It's perfect. I just wish it would never end." Sighing, I kissed my lover's chest. I felt protected by him, and I cherished that. He loved me, so the world could stop, and it would not matter to me as long as I sat next to this person for the rest of my life. I wanted to steal this moment in time, taking this with me in a special room, which was my heart. He would go to New York City with me eventually, but I would keep believing in him for now. I had to, so I could continue my life there.

"I had the most wonderful day. I have to admit, I really loved the attention... and James, wow, what a cool person; smart, young, successful, and really sweet on top of it."

"Yes, he really is. I've known him since we were kids in Switzerland. We had some crazy nights, but anytime I needed him, he was always there. This guy had my back a few times." Dominique spoke with deep admiration.

"That's great to have a friend like that. I have two loyal girlfriends in New York that are like sisters to me." I explained with admiration.

"Come what may, I'll always be here for you angel. If you need me, no matter where I am in the world, I would drop everything, I mean everything, to help you. You have my word."

Reassuring me was hard, especially when I was leaving him soon, too soon. He looked into me; I knew he meant it... At the time.

"Not to change the subject... Allie, I heard from Tory. From what I gather she is meeting you in Paris in two days. I know you are upset with everything being up in the air, but just to let you know, I have given a lot of thought to you and me. Tell me what you think. I will have my plane take you and Tory back to New York. I have a bunch of deals that I need to close here. After, I will fly over to you in a week... a week and a half at the latest. In the meantime, I will have some properties for you to look at."

Devising his plan with passion. I was thrown back, properties? Does this mean he will move to the U.S.? He saw my confusion, and so he clarified. "I want to buy an apartment in the Big Apple. If you're going to be there, well then, I have to spend time there too. I can zip across the pond when I have meetings in the EU and UK. I'll split time. When you get breaks, we can travel back to Europe. How does this sound?" Dominique lit up, talking about "our" future together. An apartment, for us?! I was flabbergasted.

"I don't know what to say! Unbelievable, this makes me so happy, love!" Crying out with joy.

"I love you, Allie. When I say something, I mean it." Leaning down to kiss me passionately. I embraced his kiss with a return of my warm wet tongue. I wanted him now. He had just turned me to mush, my heart was whole, and I was beginning to get turned on from his proximity to my heartbeat and my crazy love for him.

"Someone needs attention." Seeing my reaction to his words. "Little me." I smiled. "Let's go downstairs away from prying eyes, then we can have a nice, romantic dinner here alone this evening?" Pulling me to my feet. My privates were throbbing. I was thirsty for his cock and that strong body on mine. I felt ravenous. I needed him inside of me.

"I want you so badly," whispering as we walked to our love nest.

"Oh, Allie, I'm going to do things to you that will have you begging for more." Pulling me into our room, he looked at me wildly.

"Promise me," I begged him.

"I promise...I'll start with a spanking if you aren't careful little one." Laying me on my back as he stroked my hair. I moved my hands around on the sheets. They were silk and felt so sensual to touch. It was the perfect day, now the ideal evening to make love. I really felt like we belonged to one another, that we would stay together. I would be stronger because of my protector, my lover... My life was his now.

Dominique pulled my long sandals off and removed my

dress, exposing my breasts and my soaked, thin panties. He brushed his fingers lightly across my pussy, making me moan quietly while kissing my nipples, working his tongue to arouse them. Teasing my breasts made me even wetter. Sliding off my underwear, pushing a finger inside of me. "Oh my god," I couldn't hold back my voice. He slowly put his head between my legs, gently licking my hard clit, working me till I screamed for more.

"Take your nipples into your fingers like I do," instructing me like an experienced lover. I always did as he said, I played with my tits, and I liked it. Continuing to finger me, adding another, gazing up at me to see my reaction. I had his fingers inside of me, and I began to fuck back on his hand while he tasted my hot pussy.

"Cum for me..." He muttered while eating me out. While devouring me again, he pushed one of his fingers up, wrapping around inside. It was like nothing I had ever felt. I was weak. He was too good with my body; I had to let go; I needed to let go.

"I'm cumming... oh ...... I'm going to cum for you, baby, right now!" Screaming out, I released all over him. I was spinning from delight and lack of breathing during my orgasm. I loved it, every second of it.

"You like my tongue, don't you?" Putting his body on my frail frame, driving his hard prick slowly into me, repeating this over and over. He asked me to lay on my side, I did, and he moved back inside me, holding me tightly in his arms as we worked together in perfect harmony. His body was on fire. I could feel the blood pumping through his cock. Moving my hair away from my neck, kissing it, moaning my name.

"Allie... Allie, you are mine, Allie... Fuck I can't share you." Pulling my hips into him as hard as he could for one last pump before he filled me up. We laid there exhausted. He kept me close to him, kissing my back tenderly.

"I love you so much," he sighed.

"I know you do," teasing him.

"Smarty-pants, see that stuff will get you in trouble," lightly biting me on the neck.

"You know I love you! Darling, let's eat. I'm starving." Popping out of bed, now full of newfound energy.

"Hey you, get back here... Ok, ok, you shower off, and I'll join you in five. I've just got to lay here for a second longer."

Closing his content eyes. I was refreshed from my orgasm. What I didn't understand at the time was how tired a man would get after an orgasm, while we were completely opposite. It's so obvious now, but back then, it wasn't. I still get hungry and inspired to work after I cum. Funny, no?

I enjoyed my hot shower, smiling from the new experience. What was that little finger trick he did inside of me? I wondered what that was and the importance of it. I didn't realize then, but he had given me my first look at my "G" spot.

"Room for two?" Dominique asked, walking into the shower

room.

"Of course, but I'm getting out, love. I will go get ready for dinner." Exiting the shower, I handed him some soap.

"Not staying?" He asked.

"No can-do, baby. Besides, It takes me a lot longer to get ready." Stating the facts, as I grabbed for a fluffy towel.

"That's for sure, angel, even more so since you changed up your look," he teased.

"Ha, ha," sticking out my tongue like a toddler.

I picked out something chic-casual by Phillip Lim. A black utility belted v-neck jumpsuit with my hair pulled up, added 'no makeup, makeup' and chose to wear my emerald; I was in love, and this ring symbolized a promise between us. At least, that is what I imagined it to be. I went to the outdoor dining area to have a glass of wine, greeted by Ingrid and Roberto, our chef. She pulled a bottle of Meursault Burgundy wine, which soon became my favorite, and still is, to this day I thoroughly enjoy a good French wine. Roberto told me his choices for the menu and asked me when we would like to start dining. I told him to begin our starters in twenty minutes and then pace the dishes to enjoy. I felt decisive for once in my life, and it felt perfect. It may have just been something simple like ordering our food, but it represented leaps and bounds for me. I didn't really have choices in our homes. My mother basically told my nanny to feed me healthy, bland foods to keep me thin. Tory was afraid if I got fat, she would be embarrassed or that I would never find a husband to "take care of me." I don't know why she thought I would be looking for a man and not education; after all, she was educated. I guess she never really thought of me as bright, for that matter, I was just a thing to her, and she was a queen to me. Not for long, even queens get beheaded in history. I would sooner or later take hers, metaphorically.

Dominique entered the room with his hair a little wet, slicked back with his slight cowlick that framed his beautiful face; the man literally took my breath away.

"Hello, handsome." I couldn't wait to be close to him.

"Angel, don't you look refreshed and lovely." Kissing my hands with a cute wink.

"Why, thank you, kind sir." Feeling lucky to have this last night with him.

"What are we drinking…?" Smelling my glass.

"We have a white burgundy; would you care for one?" I implored as I raised a glass. "No, my love." Pushing it away, Ingrid appeared out of nowhere.

"Monsieur, que puis-je obtenir pour vous?" Ingrid chimed.

"Hendricks rocks with cucumber, please."

"Oui monsieur, je reviens tout de suite." Excusing herself to make his drink. Roberto, our chef, entered the room to explain the menu to Dominique and my set time frame. "Mademoiselle a demandé que le dîner commence dans vingt minutes. Cela vous convient-il, monsieur? De plus, vais-je servir le dessert que vous avez demandé?" Roberto kindly asked about our dinner and dessert.

"Oui s'il vous plaît à tous... Super!" Dominique responded with a smile. "Shall we sit? The outdoor dining area is set for us." Standing up, he reached for my hand. "Ingrid, please bring me a bottle of the 2015 Drouhin Montrachet Marquis de Laguiche Burgundy to be served at dinner and the Arkenstone as well." Dominique articulated his refined taste in wine. We sat down to our romantic night on the yacht together. Our table was full of white candles and roses; even the plates were white. Adorned with ornate, polished silver flatware, multiple wine glasses lined the table. It was a sight to be seen. It was our last night on the boat, bittersweet, I thought.

Our first course was an octopus sashimi lightly drizzled with olive oil and coarse pink salt, and tiny bits of grapefruit. It was divine, I had never had anything like this, so my mouth was in heaven. Dominique paired a 2016 Arkenstone Howell Mountain Sauvignon Blanc, which was a perfect balance of fruit for the dish. The second course was a creamy lobster risotto with tender sweet peas.

"Please open the Montrachet and pour it now. We will have it with the risotto and our main," Signaling to Ingrid, Dominique liked things just so, which took the pressure off me. I really just needed to be happy for him to enjoy us. I wish now that all of my relationships were that easy. Most men aren't like this, are they?

"Very well, sir."

"Another amazing dish, no?" Dominique spoke out in pure delight. Over the top, the perfect dishes with the more than perfect man. I really was living the life. Growing up, I wasn't allowed to have pasta or any type of rice, another fucked up dietary thing of my skinny-ass mother. "Yes, absolutely delicious," I concurred.

I turned my thoughts to spending time with him in Manhattan.

"I'm excited about your apartment in New York," grinning from ear to ear.

"It's our apartment Allie, not mine, ours, ok." He clarified.

"Yes, our apartment. Which part of the city do you like?" Researching his taste was important.

"I think I am better-suited uptown; I was thinking about 432 Park Avenue. Have you heard of it?" Questioning an NYC girl about Manhattan is like asking a fish if they like water.

"Yes, I have! It's the highest residential building. A friend of mine's father has a place there. It's overlooking all of Central Park." Telling him about the space, he loved what he heard about the amenities.

"Yes, well, I was going to wait to surprise you, but there are two in the building that are for sale. I would like you to have a look for us." Cajoling as he poured me more wine. "You've been looking for us already?!" Jumping up, I grabbed Dominique by the shoulders, kissing him lightly on the mouth.

He conceded, "yes, I can't lie; I have for the last few days. I want the best for you, angel."

"Awe, sweetheart, we're really doing this?" Delirious with his sweet words. He was looking at this place, one of the most exclusive buildings in the city!

"The apartment is somewhere around 10,000 square feet. Big enough for you?" Teasingly playful as he put his glass in the air to make a toast. "To us and our new home."

"To our new adventure," clinking his glass, watching him light up from my happiness. I'm utterly in love with this man. My everything at the time, I couldn't see anything. I was blind to any flaws he might have had. Nothing ever lasts forever. It was only a matter of time before everything would blow up right before our very eyes. I didn't know what was coming, but I was surely enjoying the ride.

We had a whole Mediterranean sea bass cooked in a thick layer of salt for our third and main course. The presentation was jaw-dropping, seeing this massive fish. Roberto chose to accompany the fish with a local favorite called ratatouille. As quickly as the fish hit the table, so did the rain. Our table quickly got hit with a pounding storm. Dominique pulled me inside; the staff grabbed the dishes and wine with light speed, bringing it inside to the formal dining room. They worked quickly to set up, and we were all noticeably wet. Dominique and I laughed.

"It came out of nowhere; that can happen here in the south,

mademoiselle," Roberto stated while handing us small towels. My love suggested a quick change of clothes, I followed his lead.

I went to my closet to grab something dry, pulling out an Akris sleeveless round neck sheath dress. Quickly I hand towel dried my hair, wiping a little mascara that ran. Calling through the bathroom door, Dominique agreed to meet me upstairs. "Ok, love," chirping back. My hair tended to get really wavy when it dried naturally. I didn't really like it, but I didn't have time to fix it, so I put a little hair product in it and went back upstairs.

"Your hair is so full. I didn't realize how much you had until now; you always subdue it. It's sexy." One of the things I thought was my worst attribute, and he really liked it; it was beginning to make me wonder about everything.

"Thank you, that means a lot, actually. I never thought big hair looked sexy. I thought it was too much." Mentioning it to me was sweet, but also just honest.

"You're welcome. I meant it, angel." Touching it lightly with his fingers. We discussed the apartment some more and our taste for decorating it. We both loved art. He decided that one of the rooms should be to practice my painting. I was over the top thrilled with the idea of being creative. I didn't realize that this would spark an extensive art career in my life.

"You know what we are missing?" He asked.

"No, everything is perfect," smiling back at him, I actually believed it.

"Music... I would love to listen to something, mmm what kind of music, you pick angel." Looking at me like I had the perfect song in mind. I wasn't really great at making any decisions, and now it was music, not one of my strengths, I would have to say looking back.

"I like this music my grandmother listens to. Have you heard of Ella Fitzgerald?" I shyly spoke up.

"Yes, I have, and I love your choice, Allie." Ingrid was standing by and put it on. As we enjoyed our main course, the song "Sunday Morning" came on. It's a sultry song with Ella's raspy voice.

"My love, will you do me the honor?" Standing up to take my hand.

"I would love nothing more." Popping up to my feet, we danced closely. It was a magical night, even with the rain; actually, I think the rain made it even more romantic. Nothing could really come between us; it meant everything and certainly not a silly storm. It felt right.... good...not good, outstanding, and nothing was going to get in the way.... not even Tory. I would have to keep her preoccupied in Manhattan. That wasn't going to be an easy task, but I had a reason for all of my determination; Dominique.

Finishing our slow dance, we sat, and our conversation turned to tomorrow's plan. He suggested we hike up to the top of Eze, where we could see some fantastic views. I loved the idea of getting some great photographs.

"Angel, let me take you to bed. You look exhausted."
Grabbing my hand, pulling me to my feet. I was tired. A lot had
gone on in such a short time. I now believed in fate, and part of
that destiny was Dominique. He was literally changing the path
of my course in my life. I realize this now as I write my story; he
changed everything.

"I hope you get used to having a good life because I swear to
you, Allie, I will give you the world. I love you, little one," sealing
it with a kiss as we retired to our room.

CHAPTER 17

Last Day...

It was our very last day and evening, then back to Paris. We grabbed a quick European breakfast and headed out to hike to Eze Village, a medieval town. Eze was an enchanting place to see. Its narrow, covered stone streets had great artisan shops, tasteful and unique. Eze is known for its spectacular views of the Mediterranean Sea and gorgeous ancient streets to meander through. It was home to a fabulous restaurant that Dominique pointed out on the way up.

"We are going to have a romantic, little lunch at Chateau Eze. The best views and the best food for you, angel." Wrapping his arm around me while we strolled along the ancient streets.

"Good, I'm starving," I replied.

"You, I noticed, are always hungry, but where do you put it? That's the question." Poking at me, he loved to tease.

"You might be right, love; I seem to always be a bit famished." Laughing as the words fell from my lips. We walked through the village buying a few small items from the locals and then headed for lunch.

Overlooking the sea, he had reserved an outside table on a private terrace. It was the most beautiful view I had ever seen. I sat there thinking to myself, this can't be real. I still look back on that day in my life and feel the very same thing... It could not have been real. I must have had a visual hallucination, but yes, it was, and it still lives somewhere in my heart. I know Dominique was older than me, but we seemed to fit. In French and European cultures, younger women weren't considered girls. They were young women coming of age, and it was perfectly fine to marry a much younger girl. Because he had such a gentle way, I felt that I was fine and that he had not been taking advantage of me. I just thought that I was his taste and he was mine. Would I marry him? That would have to be determined. Going home to New York would prove very interesting and highly challenging for us as a new couple in a totally different scenario. A place where I knew a lot of people and had school to attend, possibly home school if I get to work with James John's label.

Dominique would have his own jealousies and demons he would have to deal with, but my hope was that it wouldn't push him to the edge of losing us. Jealousy is an evil thing; it has made men want to literally kill me in my life, and they have. Amazing how it pushes a man to do unspeakable things.

"I guess if I like one of the apartments, we will take it?" Asking the question would lead to the answer that I desperately needed to hear or something else. Why is part of me still doubting him? I guess I still have the same doubts for other men that have been in my life. This seed got planted, or maybe I was born with that seed of not trusting the opposite sex. I know Tory was.

"I want you to love the apartment, not like it.... as you know, love is quite different. I need you to imagine your life there; restaurants, the location, the architecture, proximity to school... anything you can think of. Then if it checks all of your boxes and you love it… I will buy it for us." Explaining diplomatically as if there was a deal in place. I got his lingo. After all, I was raised by Tory. She was all business.

"Ok, I can do that. I'll be on it as soon as I return." Agreeing with him, he liked that very much. "Thank you, angel. I just want to make you happy."

Again, our last night of delicious wine, mouth-watering food, and lively conversation lasted for hours. It was a night to remember. We walked out of the restaurant where our driver and car were conveniently waiting. Dominique always had everything planned and arranged just so for us. He was very much a detailed person. Later I would learn more about his deception and control. For now, I was experiencing bliss and felt taken care of at every turn. I was a little sad to leave tomorrow, but I couldn't help but be curious to see Tory. We had been apart for what seemed like a lifetime. I had grown up in such a short time, and things would have to mature between us as well. She couldn't deny it; the facts would be right in front of her; me.

CHAPTER 18

City of Lights...to the...Big Apple

I wasn't unhappy waking up to leave, but I wasn't thrilled either. My first thought was of Tory... Would she pry and ask a million questions? As far as she knew, Dominique had an assistant take me all over France and Monaco. Tory never questioned him; she had a blast for three weeks without me. I was going to be left with someone regardless, but this way, she didn't have to pay anyone to watch me, and she got spending money out of it as well. This was a win, win for her. I couldn't wait to see the look on her face when she saw me. I was transformed; she couldn't deny me now. Little did she know that her little Allie was now a woman or very close to it.

Dominique said his farewells to the staff, in addition to giving everyone a nicely packed envelope full of cash for all their hard work.

I expressed my gratitude and said my goodbyes, including Ingrid, and promised to email her. I would always remember how kind Ingrid was to me. She helped me in such a pivotal place in my young life. Ingrid was there when I needed someone, my first foreign friend. Ironically, many years later I would end up buying her and her family a house because of such generosity.

We pulled up to Monaco Air, where we took a helicopter to our plane at Nice airport. In minutes, we were shuffled through a private area and onto Dominique's jet. I had become comfortable with this new lifestyle. I was now quite accustomed to it...very much like my mother. Except I was passionate. Money does have its privileges.

Laying on Dominique, I slept as he worked on emails. We were at the Le Bourget Airport outside of Paris when I woke up. Again, shuffled through quite easily and into our car with our driver; within ten minutes, we were on our way back to The Four Seasons for our last evening. I would see my mother shortly, but of course, she would not see Dominique. He decided to take a suite at a nearby hotel to not run into us, well her. I was feeling quite melancholy when we pulled up to the hotel. We had formed a plan to meet later after dinner for a hello and kiss goodbye.

I remember seeing his face look down at his hands.

"Allie, this is really hard for me. You know that," acknowledging his feelings.

"I know, I know, my love. For me as well." Pulling his beautiful face up to look at mine. "I am going to see you very soon in New York... right?" I added.

"Yes, yes, of course, angel, very." Leaning over, he kissed me softly on the corners of my lips and then in the center with full passion. I loved this man. It felt like we had it figured out, the two of us. Looking back, I could see him watching me walk to the hotel. I blew him a kiss, waved goodbye, and then he was gone.

I left my bags at the desk and walked into the hotel to meet with Tory. The time was here; I had my chance to make a "new impression." I walked into the bar and immediately got a glimpse of the blonde bombshell, which was of my mother. Wow, she was a sight! The devil dressed head to toe in red. Fabulous as always, she wore smart, wide-legged trousers, a plunging red sleeveless blouse, and a strappy gold heel. Tory was a vision of beauty and had the attention of a distinguished gentleman sitting at the bar. I could tell she enjoyed it because one, she was speaking to him, and two, she had a smile. Tory never talked to anyone she disliked; she said acting was for actors, not real people who knew themselves.

Tory stood while sipping on a Vodka Martini with olives. She never sat unless she had to, especially when she was drinking. She would say it wrinkled her clothes, and that was a "no, no." I knew it was a Martini because that was her "beginning of the evening drink." So she must have been sober at this point but would soon switch to expensive Champagne. It looks like we have that in common now; the love of good wine. The apple didn't fall from the tree after all. Maybe Tory and I had more in common than I could imagine. Perhaps she was doing some of my grooming back then, and I didn't even realize it.

I stood in the doorway for five minutes just watching her. It was entertaining differently now. I knew what she was doing, something switched in me, and I wasn't a child anymore. Commanding the room as I walked across the vast bar, men noticed; actually, even the women did. I was wearing an all-black fitted Tom Ford suit with a pair of red James John skull heels. Leaving the blouse in my suitcase, I opted for just the matching jacket; sex appeal and sophistication.

"Hi Tory," standing next to my mother proudly.

"Allie! Is that you?" Tory's mouth opened, quickly following up with a grin. "Your hair, makeup, clothes, wow, little lamb is all grown up. It looks like Dominique had you in the right hands for a few weeks! Good for you. Have a drink with me."

Admitting my changes most positively. She was actually pleased with me, so this is what it takes to make her notice me. I guess what it boils down to is that I have to look and act more like her. Smiling from her reaction, I knew she wasn't finished speaking, so I waited to hear what else she had to say.

"So, tell me what you were up to and how much shopping you did?" Shaking her head in amusement.

"I'm sure not as much as you!" Retorting quickly with ease teasing her.

"I don't know, little girl; you look all grown up to me. Now you definitely can't call me mom." Joking she was not, I don't remember the last time I called her mom.

"Mademoiselle, désolé de vous interrompre, puis-je vous offrir un verre de vin ou une boisson?" The bartender asked what I would like.

"S'il vous plaît, un Montrachet, si vous en avez. Merci beaucoup." I requested a glass of wine.

"Oui avec plaisir." Returning shortly in tow with a beautiful glass of the expensive French wine, the wine I had become accustomed to.

"Wow, somebody has amazing taste now as well." Tory's eyes smiled. I had pleased her once again.

"Yes, I am my mother's daughter." We both laughed, and for the first time, I felt like an equal and not her inadequate pain in the ass kid.

My mother noticed me. I adored it. Deep down, part of me always wanted her approval. I know it sounds pathetic, but it's true; I fucking love this train wreck. How could you not want her to love you? Growing up, she felt like an entity to me, not a person, a supernova kind of entity. Tory had power and beauty and she was deviously smart. I wanted to emulate here and then some. It was just a matter of time before I could fill her designer shoes. Tory would get hit with more than my pretty face. She would wish she never had me at some point.

"I don't have plans this evening; I think that we need to catch up and see how my caterpillar turned into a butterfly over the last few weeks..." Tory proposed a dinner. That was her giving me a compliment! I was over the moon at this point. A night with my mom as a girlfriend felt so right, and I was bursting inside with happiness, but I was trying to keep it cool on the outside.

"I think that sounds great, Tory." Raising my glass to hers and taking a sip of my wine, thinking to myself, this will be a fascinating evening.

"I need to make a call. Let's finish up here and go get changed. I will have the stylist from the salon come up and blow out our hair and make us pretty for our last night. After all, the room is paid for by Dominique," concluding, she turned to her drink.

I didn't respond because it wasn't a question. I don't think she would have cared about my hair if she were paying for it. My mother made her own money but rarely spent it on me. My eyes quickly turned to my drink, slamming the wine down; I know that isn't the way you are supposed to enjoy it. Still, I got a little nervous thinking about what she could possibly uncover. I wasn't a formable liar … yet. I signed the check, and we made our way to the elevator back to where it all began, in our enormously beautiful suite. Who knew what the night would hold?

CHAPTER 19

Last Night in Paris

Walking into the room to prepare for our big night out on the town, my thoughts turned to Dominique. I needed to see him before we left for New York City. I'd agreed to have dinner with Tory. I didn't really have a choice, did I? I went to a powder room to text him; he needed to know that I had dinner with my mother, most definitely, he'd be disappointed. He was, after all, coming to New York soon. There would be plenty of time for us. I mean, how often did I get to go out with my mother? Never actually. This was going to be an extraordinary evening. I really wanted to be with her for the first time in a long while. Tory was the popular girl in high school that everyone hated but secretly wanted to be.

"Lamb, can you get me a Goose Martini, dry with an olive?" Whispering as she covered her phone. I was all too happy to accommodate, as I had in the past. I think I knew how to make a Martini even before a pressed coffee. The thought of it made me laugh, shaking my head. I grabbed a small bottle of the Veuve Clicquot Rosé Champagne for me out of the mini bar and proceeded to finish Tory's drink. I walked back into the formal living room where Tory sat. Her energy was different; she wasn't happy. My first thought was, did she know? But how could she? No, that's not it. My second thought was we weren't having dinner. She's dumping me again.

"I have your drink! Anything wrong?" Delicately inquiring while handing the Martini off to her.

158

"Thank you for the drink, Allie. Is there anything you want to tell me?" Questioning me now in a more serious tone.

"Mother, I mean Tory, no nothing, why?"

"Oh, Allie, do you think I was born yesterday? Why wouldn't you tell me?" She demanded as she placed her drink down. She must have been concerned about something; she never lets a Martini leave her fingertips without at least two sips.

"What's going on? I don't know what you are talking about!" I pointed out. My cheeks started to get warm, I could feel my body temperature rising, and my stomach started doing backflips.

"You have an offer for James John's next campaign, and you didn't tell me? That is the first thing you should have led with... Allie, that is amazing!" Tory wasn't angry with me. She was the complete opposite. She even hugged me; I was speechless as she embraced me. I was utterly relieved and sunk into her for a few seconds before she pulled back from the awkwardness of touching me.

"I was going to tell you at dinner that James John liked my look. He hasn't made me a formal offer yet, though." Explaining to my mother. I don't know if she believed me or not, but that didn't matter at this point.

"Yes, he has, he contacted Dominique, and I got the letter from Mr. John's attorneys. You're about to model for one of the edgiest designers in the world! You are your mother's daughter!" Boasting like a proud parent.

Tory would later continue this admiration in my life. It turns out all I had to do was win. So, I never lost, not even to her. I guess everything I am is because of my mother. Although every time I did something substantial, she would pat herself on the back, it was hilarious. I got used to it; it didn't bother me after this. I am doing James John's campaign, and it's all because she didn't abort me... she had me. When I was around 8 years old, she once told me that I should feel lucky because she had me when everyone told her to get rid of it. It stuck in my head all through my life.

I still felt accomplished. No one could take that away from me. I was also hot and fierce; this was a game-changer. I was growing stronger and was no longer a kid. Now, when I look back, was I ever a child? No, I wasn't because I never stopped worrying about her. Is she dead? Is she hurt? I always thought that a police officer would come to my door and say Tory Hart died one day. She was a beautiful, reckless, damaged woman. Still, something about her is undeniably mysterious; it just baffles me and everyone else.

"I met James in Monaco; he was introduced to me by Dominique's people. They took me out one evening, and we bumped into James John and his entourage. He really loved my look and invited me to his flagship showroom." Explaining in detail as not to miss a thing. Tory was a stickler for facts, so I wanted to make sure I stayed with the truth, excluding Dominique, of course. "I didn't think he was serious when he told me that he wanted me for his next show," gushing from my own disbelief even while I told the story.

"Well, little girl, that is exactly what is happening, and then some. I need to get on the phone with Joel, our in-house attorney, and get him on your contract right this very minute, so dinner will be at ten instead of nine... Call the concierge and let him know to change it." Tory responded in her all-business voice.

"Thank you for doing this. I appreciate your input." Grabbing her hand in mine.

"I'm your mother... Right?" She said in a sarcastic tone. There's the Tory I know, she couldn't just be sweet, had to put a little vinegar in there. Oh well, I thought, "c'est la vie." I get to model, and what comes with that is freedom, travel freedom, and maybe even homeschooling.

My mind raced for minutes before taking a deep breath to recenter. I needed to talk to Dominique. I was missing him. I rang him on his private line, and he answered.

"Hello, angel."

"Hello, my love, I needed to hear your voice," I spoke with desperation.

"Hey, are you ok? What's going on?" Dominique was seemingly concerned.

"Tory is negotiating a contract for me with James," I stated.

"That's ok. I'm way ahead of her. Allie, listen, I already spoke to him and Tory on a conference call. You know I have your best interest at heart. I made sure I spoke to him first and told him what the contract should look like. You will get eighty percent of your money, and Tory will get twenty percent. I had to make sure she made something, or you couldn't model." Reassuring me that he had it under control.

"Ok, and what about my freedom? Do I get any of that?" Questioning him.

"As far as modeling, yes, you will need an escort, someone suitable to take you to your jobs, and that includes abroad. I again suggested someone that I trust from my team, free of charge. Tory agreed. In turn, this means we can travel together a fair amount, you understand?" Dominique explained slowly to give me time to absorb his intentions.

"Yes, I get it. I'm relieved, thank you, you have no idea... I get so scared, and it's hard for me to calm down." Confessing my weaknesses to him.

"I know, you've been through a lot. I am here for you, angel. I don't want your life to be that way anymore. I'm taking care of you from here on out. You can count on me. I love you, Allie." Dominique professed to me. His voice calmed me once again. He was there for me, and he wasn't going anywhere. We said our goodbyes and planned on meeting after my celebration dinner with my mother.

The door rang. I went to see who it was. It was a woman from the Hotel salon. "Hello, I'm Samantha. I'm here to do you and your mother's hair."

"Nice to meet you. I'm Allie. Come in; we can get started on me first." I requested cheerfully. Out with Tory in Paris, how glamorous. Samantha was a short blonde, reminiscent of the "LA" type of look. I don't think she could have been over 35 years old, yet she visibly had a lot of things done to her face. I could see pillows for lips, very unusually round high cheekbones, and her breasts were at least a DD. She was sweet, though. I kind of felt sorry for her a little. You could see she started off beautiful, but I guess the media makes you believe that this is what you are supposed to look like. One thing was for sure, I didn't feel that way, and I still don't.

Samantha began to work on my dry hair. She felt it looked great. I told her it was clean, so she suggested adding big curls and slight volume to the crown of my head, parting it off to the side. I loved her ideas; she worked my hair like a pro. She tossed it around a bit with a bit of spray. I have to say I looked terrific, reminiscent of Gisele's hair at Victoria's Secret runway shows. I was thrilled, "Wow, so beautiful!" Squealing out in excitement.

"Yes, well, what can I say? I'm good." Sam was right. She was good. Tory followed suit shortly after; she opted for straight hair, framing her beautiful facial structure. I really loved her, and her beauty made it hard for anyone not to. Shame her insides didn't meet her outsides.

I chose a white cocktail dress by Tom Ford. It was a mini, side-tied number, elegant and sexy. I felt like I finally knew what my style was, so I dressed with ease. Tory chose a sleeveless, emerald green lace dress designed by Dolce & Gabbana. Sheer, so of course, she wore a black tank dress under it. It truly was a show-stopper. I let her have this one. She knew how to make an entrance. All in all, we both looked amazing, and she really enjoyed "the new me"... for now.

Dinner was just around the corner from the Champs Elysées at Le Scéne. Chef Stéphanie Le Quellec's new joint La Scène was the talk of the town and with good reason. Having jumped ship at the Prince de Galles Hotel, Tory had to see the new place. Le Scéne had a shiny gold and mirrored bar, doused in twenties glamor. It was something out of a movie, and so was the crowd. I was definitely in the right place. The maitre-d greeted us. He must have been schooled by the hotel concierge because he was phenomenal at "ass-kissing."

"Hello, our reservation is under Hart for two," explaining to the impeccably dressed man. "Good evening ladies, you look beautiful, our pleasure to have you. Chef Stephanie is here tonight, and she will say hello later." Greeting us in broken English.

"Thank you, sir, for the compliments, and we thank you for fitting us in on such short notice. We very much look forward to meeting Chef Stephanie." Professing my admiration for the chef as I smiled at Tory with all of my teeth. I must have looked like a ten-year-old at that moment, but I was so happy to be with her. Here with her, my mother, my everything since I was a girl. For the first time in my life, I thought she loved me, me Allie!

We dined on the most fabulous dishes, drizzled with vibrant colored sauces and what looked like four-leaf clovers to finish the plates. I didn't know all of the components, but I knew I loved the art of the dish. I loved art altogether. Even when I was a small child, I took photographs with my "real" father and his fancy

Polaroid camera. The photos turned out massively interesting. The subjects were a bit odd for most, like my infatuation with cows, oh how I loved them. One time, I went to the pasture of our neighboring farm at just nine years old in the middle of the night to photograph them. One had died, and the cows had what I thought resembled a funeral. I shot it with my camera, the cows circling and mooing; it sounded like cries to me, and maybe it was. I started noticing everything like an artist that summer. It set me up for the massive career that I would later have in my adventurous life. I guess you could say it all started with a cow.

"So, Miss Hart, tell me about your three weeks in Europe. I heard you were escorted by Ingrid, Dominique's assistant?" Showing interest, she was very curious about what I was up to.

"Yes, Ingrid... she was an outstanding teacher. She helped me learn a lot about European ways, clothes, food, art, people... pretty much everything." Hesitating to not screw up and say my love's name. I told her half-truths. After all, she would have flipped if she knew all that I actually learned. The kissing and lovemaking would not have fared well with this tigress.

"Wow, Allie, that sounds all too amazing. I should have stuck around!" Half joking, she would have never stuck around with the old me, now the new one, maybe.

The waiter chimed in. There was a new guest at the table; to our surprise and delight, Chef Stephanie.

"Thank you for returning to our restaurant. I have not seen

you since we left The Prince de Galles location." Chef Stephanie smiled as she shook my mother's hand.

"With pleasure, we come for you... not the location, and always will. You are the very best." Complimenting the chef in her convincing manner.

"One day, I hope to be able to cook half as well as you. I love the creativity of your plating as well, so imaginative." I added.

"Thank you for the generous compliments, young lady. Try, and you will succeed at anything you put your mind to." Chef Stephanie said her goodbyes and then had the waiter send over several desserts. As well as two lovely, long-stemmed, petite glasses of Mirabelle plum liqueur. The plum alcohol was perfect for after dinner and sweet on my lips. It made my stomach warm and also my head a bit light.

"Let's chat a little about the James John contract. It's quite lucrative, that is if you follow through with your obligations. Allie, this is business, not a game. Other models have been known to get into all kinds of shit, which ruins their reputations. I mean, look at Kate Moss. I know she's successful and still works, but damn the drug gossip and so on about her. This type of behavior doesn't help. It hurts. A lot of ladies spoil their careers by fucking off. Do you understand, we can't have this happen? It boils down to you; you have an opportunity to make a lot of money and be fiercely independent......well, you still have to finish school but to have a career. This real career makes you a small fortune." Tory loved to preach and hear herself speak, so I nodded my head and just let her. After all, there was no stopping this lady.

"I get it. I'm not going to get messed up on drugs or anything... I promise you." Pleading with her is what she wanted so I did, then it subsided, she became boss, and I let her. It was in "my" best interest to keep her on my side.

"Good to hear, Allie. I can trust you to do the right thing. I know I haven't always been the best mom, but I provided for you, and ... you know what I'm saying, right?" Stumbling over her words as if she had feelings for me. Was this my mother trying to be human? I was utterly taken aback. Who was this woman before me? Wow, maybe she does have a heart, I thought as I looked at her concerned face. Then the other Tory reared her ugly head. "You know I don't fucking understand this "protection" clause that Dominique put in your contract. Where the hell does he get off protecting you... from me?" She ranted and raved about the logistics of it all. I didn't answer.

I just waited for her drink to kick in. I was floored by this turn of events; all of the good flew out the doors of the beautiful restaurant. I was deeply saddened. I felt like crying my eyes out. I didn't, but instead, I excused myself and went to the ladies room. I could hear her mumbling under her voice as I left.

"Pull it together, Allie... damn it, why does she have to be such a cunt?" I soon regained composure and remembered Dominique loved me, which is why he put the clause in. Tory was just pissed because she didn't have complete control over my money or me. Dominique gave her just enough to keep her on the hook. Allowing me to model benefitted her just enough. This newfound career would take me places, and I couldn't wait to go there.

I sorted myself and returned to the table. Tory was back to being pleasant.

"I might have overreacted. Let's go back to the hotel and get some sleep. We have an early flight in the morning." Tory acknowledged her temper for the very first time in my life. It was a small gesture, but I was still surprised. How confusing she was, even more so now. I was used to her ignoring me, and now I was in her spotlight. I hoped that this was a sign, that things would only get better.

Returning to our suite, Tory excused herself and retired to her room. Either she truly was tired, or she wanted to make various calls to her minions; my guess was the latter. I never saw that coming. I would have thought she would have gone to the bar to see about a drink or a man. She was the most undeniably fantastic flirt. I mean, I would have flirted with her if I were an eligible bachelor. I say this as a joke, of course.

I texted Dominique as soon as I heard the door close. He called instead of writing me back. I was pleasantly surprised.

"Hey you, I'm so happy you called!" Gushing into the phone.

"Angel, it's so good to hear your voice," he replied.

"Oh, you have no idea. I miss you already!" I conceded.

"Allie, go to the door and open it. I have something sitting outside of your door," he instructed. I ran over to the door, opening it quickly and to my surprise... There he was, my love, standing in front of me with just a single yellow flower, just like the one he gave me at the airport, on the very first day I met him. My handsome, sexy, first love. Overwhelmed, I began to cry. Tears of joy filled my big eyes, streaming out while I busted out in a laugh.

"Come here, you make me want to cry when I see that." Pulling me in with one hand while gently wiping my face dry.

"Come on. I want to show you something." Dominique explained while dragging me to the elevator.

"Where are you taking me?" Whispering in his direction. He didn't answer as he pulled me into the empty elevator. The doors closed, and he began kissing me passionately. I was all too receptive and got lost in the moment when the doors opened; we were in the lobby.

"I think we should get out." Dominique joked.

He scooped me in his arms as we walked outside. A driver stood waiting in a midnight blue sapphire Rolls Royce Phantom.

"After you..." Dominique opened the door and then quickly ran to the other side like a kid. He kissed me intensely like he had not seen me in a year. I felt the same way. I was beyond thrilled to be with my gorgeous man. My heart was whole; it was as though the world around us could just fall away, leaving nothing except for him and me. I could see nothing else.

We pulled up on a quiet narrow street with a dull light.

"Why the odd red light, my love?" Curiously questioning.

"It's a private club, invite-only, very exclusive," he explained to me. He had to do a lot of that. I knew there were only speakeasies and private members, but I never got to go to one till now. We walked up to a large white man with a funny handlebar mustache. He stood guard in front of the scarlet velvet drapes, where we would enter. Dominique announced himself as we passed by quickly. We walked into a low-lit lounge with four red and black, round banquets filled with people and around twelve bar stools lined with a gold and black bar full of mirrors. The chandelier lighting was also a hue of red, so the entire place had a sexy vibe. It was small but appeared so much larger because they didn't allow people to stand. They had a complete set of rules on a blackboard in red type, and that was one of them. There was only one banquet left, and that was ours. He reserved an intimate spot for us to enjoy one another's company for a few hours before I had to return and rest for the day of travel.

"Angel, what do you think?" His lips touch my ear, bringing a chill through my body.

"It's so red... sexy. I love it!" I brought my lips to his hand, kissing it while I stared up at him intently. I wanted him to know how much I appreciated him. I still remember Dominique looking back at me with such feeling. He adored me for that, for all of my little gestures of admiration I showered him with.

I had never seen anything like this. I only heard about places like the lounges in Manhattan, but this was another secrecy level. Only living in Manhattan for a few years, I wasn't like the other girls my age. They were all knowledgeable and went to nightclubs at fourteen years old. I would have been murdered if I had done that. I also didn't want to. I liked art, cooking and my books. I enjoyed my camera, Central park for explorations. I also liked boys, but they didn't notice me, but that was all changing. I was a woman or at least looked like one. I would model for a top designer. Everyone would know my name and my face. I wanted to pinch myself; I couldn't believe my life. I'm sitting in one of the most exclusive establishments in Paris with a man that jumped off the covers of GQ. I prayed it would never end. I begged God to not let anything ruin the beginning of something great; us. My happiness was hard to contain. I felt alive for the first time in my entire life. I, Allie, a sexy, intelligent, and now a businesswoman.

Our head mixologist enjoyed some hand-crafted cocktails; yes, bartenders now have fancy titles. One because they deserve it, two because they truly mix up potions for our delight. I loved the cherry fruit they paired with our bourbons; it was warm and had a sweet syrup finish. Enjoying the taste of whiskey on his breath in the past was different than this evening. Tonight it was sweeter; kissing him more deeply brought flavors from his mouth into mine. The drink turned a key, I got aroused, and my pussy was dripping on my seat. He could always tell when I was turned on. Sliding his hand up my dress, he began to massage my sweet spot from the outside of my panties. I moved his hand gently to the inside of my underwear.

"Oh, you are a bad girl," he smirked.

"I'm your bad girl."

Teasing him was now the norm. I had learned a lot from my teacher.

"Yes, you are... forever," Dominique corrected me, changing the tone of his voice; he got serious. "Allie, just be good when you get back to New York. I don't want to have to worry about you." Pleading with me not to hurt us. Why would he feel this way? I pulled back a bit.

"Do you not trust me?" I asked.

"I trust you; I just don't trust everyone else. I need you to be aware. Most people aren't out for your best interest. I am Allie... your fucking mother isn't, and every guy in New York City isn't!" Now, what did I do? He was angry with me... for what? I was beyond confused.

I had to fix it. I couldn't have this tension between us.

"I love you... I'll be careful. I am back to school in a week, and now I'll be working with James. I won't be in places like this without you, promise. Please, you have to believe me. I'm listening. I understand your concerns." Explaining desperately as I grabbed his face in my hands. He melted into my arms like a child; his broad shoulders collapsed. I had said the right thing. I felt good, actually powerful. This was the first time I told a man "what he needed to hear," and this would not be the last time I had to do this. I started understanding men and women and fed off words like a sweet cake. It made me think, then smile while I held him on my breasts. Dominique was letting me fly out of the nest and was feeling vulnerable; at the time, I didn't know just how much.

"Let's finish this. I have something else to show you,"

Dominique prompted.

"As you wish, I'm yours, so take me where you like," I conceded. He paid quickly and got us back into the car. We were back at the hotel.

"Dominique, this is your surprise?" Joking, but I knew him by now. He would have something planned; it was in his nature to be in control at all times. Tapping me on the ass to move me into the elevator, "get in there." He pushed up against me. I could feel his semi-hard penis.

We got off on a PH floor, and I quickly realized this wasn't my floor.

"Darling, where are you taking me?" I asked, but he did not answer. Pulling me down a long, opulent hall of gold to a set of double doors marked "Penthouse." I was dumbfounded; he must have read my face because he laughed. I still had this girl in me, no matter how much makeup I applied to my face.

"You like?" He kissed my hand.

"Je t'aime, my love," I replied.

"My little French American girl. I like it when you speak French. It's cute," teasing me like a boy. "Oui je sais mon petit poulet," I agreed and made up a little nickname for him.

"You're hysterical Allie, little chicken?" He howled.

Walking around the rooms was more fabulous than the next, especially the bath. Wow, it was enormous, with stunning views from the windows around it. You could actually see the Eiffel Tower from the tub!

"Darling, please come outside." Calling out from the balcony, he looked like a dream, his tall frame and the backdrop of one of the most fucking romantic cities in the world. I was literally losing my mind with delirium. I followed his voice as it disappeared around the corner of the enormous space to an outdoor garden of flowers. He had arranged a small table for two with candles and Champagne.

The whole place faces the brilliant lights of the tower and all of Paris itself. After reading the book called "The Little Princess," I saw a movie. This movie had the same feel, but it was a genie making her wishes come true in the story. For me, it was Dominique. I couldn't imagine a more perfect moment in my time. It was magical. Dominique stood behind me with his arms wrapped around my waist. We shared a beautiful moment looking at the city of lights.

"I wanted to make your last night special," he whispered into my ear.

"You exceeded any expectations, my love." Turning to him, I placed my arms around his neck. His beautiful blue eyes were full of possibilities, I reached up to meet his full mouth, pressing on his lips for what seemed like an eternity.

Sincerely he returned my kiss with gratitude, even more passionate than anything I had ever felt from him. We didn't even open the Champagne yet, and we were already thinking about pleasing one another. Within minutes we were heading to a king-size bed of silk.

"Show me, Dominique, show me my love..." Begging for it.

"What, what is it you want to see?" He teased, knowing I wanted him inside of me. He could see the desire in my eyes. "You want this?" His eyes lowered as he rubbed the outside of his pants. I could see his hard cock. I didn't want to wait any longer to have it. I removed my shoes, slowly moving onto the bed. He removed his shirt; afterward, he pulled me off the bed.

"Let me take this off. I want you naked," ordering me while he slid my dress over my shoulders. I was exposed, no bra, just a tiny thong filled with excitement. Dominique sat me on the bed while spreading my legs. I gladly let him guide me. I wanted his hot tongue so badly on my enlarged clit. I could feel the blood rushing all over my body, tingling, pushing me to cry out his name.

"My love, please," I moaned as he pulled off my panties, pushing me down on the bed. Spreading my legs even wider as he put his warm lips onto my pussy, working my mound until I was dripping wet. He put his fingers in me at the same time, fucking me softly as he worked it. Just as I felt like I would release, he stopped, stood up, and pulled his pants off, exposing his sizable hard manhood. He was proud of it. He held it firmly as I licked my lips.

Laying on my craving frame, entering me the first time was the best; he let out loud cries of pleasure. Fuck, it felt like heaven.

Thrusting me like a gladiator, over and over again. We were in perfect harmony as I raised my hips, wrapping my legs tightly around his hot, muscular body. Moving like lovers now...we were great lovers.

"I fucking love you, Allie, you know that. You have to belong to me, only me."

Forcing himself further into me, so deep that it hurt, but even the pain caused pleasure for us. "I do......I do, my love," conceding with delights beyond comprehension. My swollen clit was hitting his body, and his hard cock was driving me to heaven.

"I don't want to cum yet, Allie," crying out as he moved out of me and wrapped my legs around his head. Positioning himself back down on my wet pussy, he began to massage my privates with his tongue. He only had one goal: to hear me cum on his face. He wouldn't let up until I gave into him. I couldn't hold back much longer. I was at my threshold, losing my grip on reality. Pushing his tongue hard one last time, creating a flood of ecstasy all over his beautiful face.

"Oh my God, oh my God!" Surrendering to him, I cried out the most exquisite orgasm. He knew what he had done to me. He could feel the hot liquid.

"I love hearing that sound and that taste. You taste so fucking good." Entering me with pure desperation. Thrusting over and over again until he couldn't. "Allie, I'm cumming, angel, I'm cumming inside of you." Melting onto my limp body. I was in love with this man, I would do anything to make him happy, and he would do anything to keep me.

We were bonded now. What about the future? What would that hold for us? Tired from lovemaking, we fell asleep in one another's arms, entwined by our legs. Knowing that I had to leave before Tory got up made me a little nervous, so I woke up around 4 am. The idea of leaving him felt wrong, but I knew New York was there waiting, and I had to go. A part of me wanted to return as the new Allie to my big city. I admired him while he slept; he looked unearthly; divine. I imagined a life with him as I leaned over his beautiful body. I couldn't see myself in the future with anyone but him. I curled into his chest for a couple of more peaceful hours before I had to leave him.

My lover woke me with some tea, and his usually tickles my nose.

"Angel, you have to get up now. You have a flight soon," kissing me on my breasts.

"Ok, my love, I'm up... don't do that, or I will be forced to stay." Whining, I threw the sheet over my eyes.

"Yes, but I will see you in just two weeks, promise. You have a lot to do for us there. I'm counting on you to look at the apartment," coaxing me to my feet to get dressed. I woke, knowing all would be alright for me in New York City, but I only hoped it would be for us. I got dressed and made my way to the door. Dominique walked with me.

"I love you, Allie, don't forget that. You've captured my heart." Bending down for that one last kiss. The kiss was intense and soft. I could feel his love for me.

"I love you. My heart would explode if I loved you anymore, you know that right?" Reassuring him one last time before I left. I knew he needed that. I was beginning to understand men. I gave him a long hug, walking backward to the elevator while he watched in amusement.

I went to my mother's suite, packed, showered, and changed quickly. I heard Tory on the phone in another room. She was making some sort of deal and was really pissed off. My fear was that she would take it out on me the entire way back. Why would she pick fights, probably just to browbeat me? I guess her mother did the same to her.

"Hello and good morning Allie," peeking into my room, I wondered if she knew I wasn't here last night.

"Hi, how did you sleep?" I asked.

"Very well, thanks. I canceled the commercial flight to New York." Happy in her response. "Why? What's going on?"

Baffled by her words...were we staying?

"Well, Dominique sent me a message this morning. He offered his jet to us. I, of course, said yes. Who wants to fly commercial, when you can fly private... and let's not forget free Champagne?" Explaining with enthusiasm. I wonder why he did that, I knew, but she had no idea.

"That's so sweet of him," mumbling to myself as I packed. Dominique's generosity was no longer shocking to me. I knew this was part of my life now. I was grateful but not too surprised. Men in my life would continue to do things for me. It seemed to me, if I stayed somewhat innocent, or at least appeared so, they would continuously give.

We left the hotel with an enormous amount of designer bags. She didn't mind that the "assistant" took me shopping. After all, we wore the same size; it only benefited her. Settling on the expansive plane, we could unwind and have some fun on our six-hour ride to The Big Apple. "Allie, I need to speak to you about your newfound career." Already she started back on me about this. We didn't even take off yet.

"Sure." What else could I say? I was still her daughter. I had to hear her words, whether I liked it or not. Tory had her "intimidating" face on; she could be scary when discussing business.

"You signed with the James John Brand, that's brilliant, but we need to talk about the best modeling agents in Manhattan. We also need someone with a long enough reach for Europe, Asia, and North America. James John is a global brand. His face should be as well; you... Keep your schedule open for me. I will be sending you out to meet a few people immediately upon arrival. We need to get your house in order Allie. Got it?!" She went on and on about the modeling business and a list of wild requests for me to do. One was even attending a seminar on how to think like a man. She's clearly insane...think like a man? The last thing I wanted to become was a man or a woman like her. For argument's sake, I politely agreed to do anything she wanted of me. After all, I knew she had a head for business, even when she was completely annihilated.

The flight was longer than I expected, more so because she would not let up on me about work. I had a sick feeling that modeling wouldn't be as fun as I expected, not if she was running my career. I was so young, but I knew that I didn't want her in charge of my every move. Something needed to be done, but what? I wished I could live on my own.

CHAPTER 20

Mad-Hattan

We walked into our smallish penthouse for two on 82nd and Park. It was around 3,000 square feet, and came with magnificent views of Central Park. I felt lucky to have this home, it was smaller than my two best friends, but I felt much more relaxed. My mother had fantastic taste, so the apartment reflected that. All of our furniture was Casamilano. Tory would say, *"it was understated Italian furniture design of the highest quality. Which, equally, respected the environment, and that the curving lines mimic the lines of the body".* The sofa and chairs were light, tons of white and beige. The lamps, all the accents were gold and rust colors. The only thing that really jumped out was our art. Tory would often say - "Art should be the first thing you notice in a home." I loved art, so I would tend to agree. We had a Basquiat, Picasso, and a Damian Hirst dot painting. I liked Damian's work, and hoped to meet him someday. He was outspoken and rude to the galleries, he broke barriers, and I admired his tenacity.

My bedroom, my sanctuary, was white, except for my headboard, a soft rose color. My room looked like a child's. It needed an update. I loved my own space though, it was a safe place, where I could be locked away, not be seen or see her. My fabulously messy mother.

There was a sizable dining room where I would work on projects or assignments from school since we ate out almost every night, or at least she did. I would sometimes meet my friends at places like Serafina for pizza or at Phillipe Chow for expensively priced Asian cuisine. I lived Uptown; therefore, I stayed Uptown... for now. I didn't share the same excitement for an Upper East Side apartment with Dominique. I preferred to try the Downtown scene since it was young and livelier. I wanted to be in the thick of it. I never really felt like a part of the society up here on the park. It was much stuffier and just old to me. I dreamed of buying something in Tribeca, near Beyonce and Jay-Z, not living next to Donald Trump. Don't get me wrong, I was still grateful. I didn't complain about much at this point. I now thought life was possible, not to endure, but to enjoy and have love for once in my life. All for me, Allie Hart. I would often get sad, feeling like the world was at high speed and I was in slow motion trying to catch up.

I imagine this is how Tory feels all the time. Sometimes I would get to the point where I would pinch myself just to make sure I was alive. Now, my mind was racing at lightspeed.

"Hey kid, make me a Grey Goose Martini, dirty." My mother opened my door with her request.

I just got to my room, where I began to unpack my amazing new clothes. I had a new wardrobe, hair, makeup, and attitude. I was ready to call my friends to reconnect. After all, we had four days before it was back to "all-girls" school.

"Sure, Tory, can I have one?" Yelling down the hall as she walked away.

"I don't care, have whatever you want..." As she got back on her cell for another call. I could hear her back at it, discussing me and my contracts with her lawyer. I think she became obsessed with it. Tory was very much determined to secure her position and profits in the "Allie Show."

I brought her drink to her bedroom, where she was lounging in a sitting area. She enjoyed her loveseat and chairs in front of a large window that faced Central Park. This is where she would make her "ball-busting deals" from. Tory was a fan of opulence, so her accents of pillows and throws were all gold Hermes, and the smell of rosewood streamed out of her doors as you would approach. So rich...so her. The lilac silk bedding from ABC downtown was ridiculously priced, but Tory would say that "you spend half your time in bed, so it should be the best one." When she wasn't around, I would often go into her room and smell her bed pillows. They smelled like her, beautiful. I often wondered how this woman was so perfect as a shell, but the insides reminded me of nothingness. I didn't want to be like that, but eventually, something would switch in me, and I would have no choice in my life but to change.

"Allie," I heard her calling me once again. I knew when she hung up, the trial would continue. "Yes, Tory," I answered.

"Why don't you join me for a drink?" She was up to something; I could clearly see that her niceties were fake. We both took a sip, and she began, as I knew she would. Funny, I thought, this woman hasn't spoken to me this much ever. Our conversations in the past lasted maybe five minutes on the norm.

"I just got off the phone with Joel, my attorney, and I feel that your contract should read an even split of 50-50 between the two of us. After all, I will have to manage your career and make arrangements for staff. Dominique has worked it at twenty. That just doesn't sit well with me...after all, I will have to take time out of my career to help with yours, to ensure I protect my daughter. Don't you agree?" Demanding, I take her words into high consideration. I had no time to disagree or agree. Why did she even ask me? I didn't interrupt. I just sipped on my Martini and began daydreaming about this evening...hmmm, what could I get up to with my girlfriends? What should I wear? They had always wanted me to look more like them, womanly. I was reeling inside; I wanted to call them. I periodically would chime in with a grunt. This made her feel like she had my attention.

Finally! She let me speak.

"I'm so sorry; I kind of think twenty is fair. Besides, I don't need you to babysit me. I can hire my own attorney, tutor, and agent with the money I make. Also...I thought it would be a good idea to let Dominique's people handle my business since they got the campaign in the first place." Countering bravely with my opinions. I was entirely in charge of what I said, and she was quiet until I finished.

"Listen to me closely; Dominique will not handle anything for you, got it! I am your mother, and what I say goes. You think you're all grown up now, you want to try it your way... fine. Find your own tutor, but your attorney comes from my firm. I will look at all contracts that come through and set the appointments for the agents that I think are suitable. Allie, understand this, if you fuck it up... then, I take over, and the scale tips towards me." Tory was pissed, but she actually let me win this one. That was a massive thing for me. I got her respect for the first time, well, what appeared to be so.

I left her and went back to my safe place; my room. I called my friends Serena Tillman and Beth, Hollingsworth, who came from a very waspy society. They were from extremely wealthy families, old money. Their homes were gaudy and super-sized, so they loved coming over to mine. They enjoyed rummaging through Tory's closet as soon as they walked in. I never minded because Tory didn't really pay attention to everything she had or spent. She converted a guest room into her closet. Needless to say, it was huge, fucking fabulous, but we wouldn't expect less from her. We had made a plan to meet up around eight o'clock at my place. Tory was heading out early for a dinner date and some party. She most likely wouldn't be back till late, if at all.

My friends were on time; I knew that because I heard them yelling my name repeatedly as they ran down the hall to my room.

"Hey you, get your ass over here, let me take a look at you," howling, Serena grabbed me and swung me around. "What the fuck Allie, you look fucking amazing!" Trailing behind her was Beth; she was undeniably in shock over my transformation.

"What, nothing's changed."

Giggling with happiness, I'm finally with my besties. I love these two so much. I couldn't wait to fill them in on every tiny detail. That's what girls do. Of course, shortly after they arrived, we headed right for the wine refrigerator. They always had free reign at my place, my mother didn't care, and I let them drink whatever they wanted. After all, we had unlimited alcohol in our place. Their parents were much stricter, considering mine were non-existent. It really wasn't a good comparison.

"Let's open some rosé Champagne!" I insisted.

"What! Allie, you've changed, you never drank before... wow, you have a lot to tell, don't you?" Grabbing the bottle from my hands, Serena began ripping away at the foiled top.

"Yea biatch, and your hair, make-up, clothes ... it looks like you went to a designer, finishing school!" Tickling me, Beth was dying to know everything. I had become everything she tried to encourage me to be. I guess I just wasn't on the same wheel she was.

"Come on, I wasn't that bad."

I joked, but they were right, I was a changed person, and I felt fierce. We were back together, and I couldn't wait to soak it all up. I was different; I wanted to see everything through my new eyes. My friends always took care of me and encouraged me to be braver, but I didn't get it. Grabbing the bottle, and running into my room, I was dying to show my friends my new clothes. We all tried them on together. I agreed to let them wear some, why not, they're just clothes. They were kind enough to stick around for some really fucked up shit in my home. Beth had found me multiple times hurting. The one that resonates is when she came over to my place and found me on the floor of my bathroom, face covered in blood. Tory had pushed me down, busting my head open. I lay in it till my friend arrived to help. Beth never told a soul and cleaned me up like a good sister while crying with me. She was my protector, no one messed with me. Believe me, they tried. After all, I was a nobody from Pennsylvania when I came to Sacred Heart, the elitist girls' school for the well-bred and wealthy clans of New York City. A jungle of egos and bitches. Beth Hollingsworth loved me from the moment she met me. I didn't understand that exactly, but I was thankful to have a friend that had my back.

Beth was a beautiful petite brunette, with wide brown eyes, with doll-like features; fragile to look at, yet commanding when she spoke. I used to call Beth the defender. I thought she would make a great attorney like her father or a politician like her granddad. Still, Beth later became all of the above. Serena was goofy, blond, bubbly, with big blue eyes, and always slightly high from edibles. Although she was petite, she was a force, a boss that took zero shit from anyone. She said she had to microdose" to get through her life at home. Needless to say, Serena was always happy. They were a bit smaller than me in height but wore the same size. This was good for them, but not so much for me.

"Where should we go tonight?" Jumping up and down from my buzz.

"One second, first, let's make a toast to Allie and her new look!" Raising her glass, Beth insisted on entwining our glasses. It was our thing, corny, but our specialty. So we always remembered.

"Woohoo, go Allie, go Allie, it's your birthday, and we're gonna party like it's your birthday!" Serena sang loudly. She was a wild child; this hot petite blonde was not stopping. She was the kind of girl you would have to drag off the table.

Deciding to all wear different colors, but of course, not to clash. I wore a white knit dress with silver embroidery. I paired it with a simple red-bottom beige pump. I styled my hair wavy and parted in the middle, very Charlie's Angels. I was feeling it. Serena had a slicked-back high pony, opted for gold, shiny, sparkly Chanel, and Beth had straight long hair off to the side. She went for a black Tom Ford v-neck fitted dress. We looked pretty impressive and felt even more so after the second bottle of Champagne.

"I have a fucking dope party downtown for us. We have to go; the guys are really tight. I know the host, so let's go!" Dancing with her devilish smile, Serena had all of the ins. I went along with whatever they said most of the time, but that would change in the very near future.

"If it's lame, we go somewhere else, ok? I have our names on a couple of lists," adding in her bossy nature, Beth was definitely the head of the girl pack. I went to the lounges, but I always stayed hidden behind them. I didn't like alcohol at the time, had no confidence, but tonight was game on. I couldn't wait to get out. I was now outgoing and confident; I felt totally different.

Serena sent for an Uber driver, and we headed to the lobby.

"Allie, little Allie, is that you?" Walter, our doorman, ran behind me.

"Yes, Walter, it's me." We all laughed.

"Europe did wonders for you, miss!" He said sweetly. We giggled, but Walter saying that made me smile, and I thanked him for that. Doormen in New York should write their own books. They see some fucked up shit, 100 percent.

Jumping into the car, we headed to this mystery party that Serena suggested but clearly knew nothing about.

"Look ladies, all I know is this guy's apartment we're heading to is owned by some famous economist's son, who happens to be a baller on Wall Street and is supposed to be hot as fuck!" Laughing as she explained her findings. She rarely would steer us wrong.

"Ok, good enough for me." I concurred.

"It better be cool, or we're leaving!" Beth warned with a half-smile. She loved to bust on Serena; it was their thing.

We arrived in front of a renovated historical building downtown, which looked pretty dope. Inside were massive lofts known for housing actors, rappers, models, and obviously Wall Street superstars. I was excited to see what this was going to be like. After announcing ourselves to the doorman, we were sent into the elevator, but after getting out, we had to take a second, which was private and only for the penthouse. This was it. I was beaming; I felt like it was my coming out party. Allie as a woman, not some wallflower no one noticed.

CHAPTER 21

That Knight, Heavenly Knight

We walked off the elevator, and to our delight, there was a fantastic loft full of hot people. A-listers from the movies, music, and good-looking people everywhere. This party was something out of Who's Who in Manhattan. Heading towards the bar, we sized up the room and looked around to see if we could find a person that knew who the "hot" bachelor was that owned this place. This had the bones of a historical loft, but ultra-modern white Roche Bobois furniture and Chihuly chandeliers, silver accents everywhere, and even white marble floors lined the vast space. We were at the right place; it couldn't have been better, or could it?

"Allie, baby! Is that you?" Raph, no, it couldn't be. It was as though everything went blank in the world; all I could see was his face. I must have stood there for fifteen seconds staring at him before I spoke; I was in shock.

"Raph? You're here, what? Umm... what are you doing here?" Stumbling over every word that fell from my lips. Beautiful Raph. This is precisely what Dominique did not want to happen. Yet, here I am in the middle of a crowded New York apartment with him, someone I undeniably have feelings for. Oh my God, he's here.

Beth could see my face and came over to save me... "Allie's first time speaking. Hi, I'm Beth. You are...?" Extending her hand out to Raph.

"Hello, I'm Raph. I'm a friend of Allie's; we met in St. Tropez," shaking her hand with his radiantly charming smile.

My friends were chatting it up with him for some time about the Riviera and where we met. The entire time he locked onto me, I could feel his piercing green eyes driving directly inside of me, almost like he could see my heart pounding out of my chest. I shouldn't have reacted towards another man, but I did. Part of me hated myself. The other felt relieved. I could finally have a moment with this guy I found so striking and charming without the fear of getting caught.

"Hi!" Interrupting my friends, finally saying something normal. This time with more confidence than I had shown when we first arrived. My friends got the hint and excused themselves; they could see the obvious connection.

"Let's find the owner; he's got to be around here somewhere," turning away, Serena was determined to locate him.

"Hi, do you know where the host is?" Beth asked a couple standing close by.

"Yes, it's Raph. You were just talking to him."

Serena in the meantime would get high on cocaine. Beth hated that she did that shit and was always trying to stop her. I knew only time could fix Serena's little problem. Eventually, she got married and that phase was over, but that didn't happen for quite some time. I wasn't in the headspace to judge or be judged, so I just loved her for who she was.

"How do you know the host?" Questioning Raph, I couldn't help but move closer to him. "You're looking at him." Responding, his words were in slow motion to me. The fullness of his mouth made me want to pounce like a wild cat. This man had the most welcoming smile, he would light up a room, and his cockiness was funny. He had just enough to make him charming. I loved his full wavy black hair. It was neatly pushed back on the sides, but the top was all over, sexy, I thought, just sexy.

"Oh, that's funny; in a million years, I would have never thought I would bump into you on my first night back." Shaking my head in disbelief. I was flirting with him. The only thing I was thinking about was how much I really wanted to touch him. That was short-lived. My mind began to race... Snap out of it, Allie! You can't be so dismissive of your love for Dominique. I had to be loyal to him; he's committed to me and has helped me so much, I owe him everything.

"I'm sorry, I should find my friends... Can we chat some more later?" Politely excusing myself, I was confused and needed to clear my mind.

"Sure, Allie, but your friends are having a good time. They can stand to be away from you for a minute, no?" Pleading like a kid, almost too hard to resist him. I smiled and walked away. "Allie, baby, you are breaking my heart... love hurts," yelling behind me, everyone turned to look at who he was talking to. It was flattering. It made me feel important. This hot piece of ass, not only desirable but intelligent, rich, and funny, professing his love. I liked it. I adored his attention. He made me feel different than Dominique; he was younger and less serious. I felt something for him, I just didn't know what to do, but I would figure it all out in time. This wasn't the end of our story. I knew that.

The night was pretty fucking cool. The DJ, David Guetta, was there and spun for thirty minutes; it must have cost a fortune. The place was on fire; it got louder as the music got more intense. We danced, drank and drank some more. I was so happy to be with my girlfriends. Our wolfpack would see many more nights like this; I was a new person. I wanted to have fun...finally.

As promised, I went to say goodnight to Raph. He was speaking to an attractive dark-haired girl, so I wasn't sure if I should interrupt, so I quickly turned and walked away. He noticed, "Allie, please come over here. I want you to meet someone." Pulling on my arm, I agreed and turned with a smile. "Allie, this is my other favorite girl, Jenna. Jenna, this is Allie, my future girlfriend." Staring at me with his wicked smile.

"Hi Allie, I'm his sister, the mature one," extending her hand to me. I was so relieved... his sister! "Hello, it's really nice to meet you." We chatted for a few minutes, and Jenna excused herself; again, we were alone.

I needed to say my goodbyes as well.

"I should get going. It's been a long day for me." I pointed to my watch.

"Can I see you again?" Raph stepped closer to me, looking down on me. His face was close enough to touch. He made me uncomfortable. I felt like I needed to kiss him. It was hard for me; Raph was like my kryptonite...I was weak. My thoughts made me feel a little guilty. I looked down so that I wouldn't have to look into his sultry eyes.

"I'll walk you out." Touching my shoulder, I felt a thousand chills throughout my body. What the fuck is happening to me?

"No, that's ok, stay and enjoy your party...I will grab Beth and Serena." I removed his hand, slowly backing away from his proximity.

"Ok...you know I'm not going to stop, right. I know you like me as much as I do you. Something happened in Europe, and you know it, Allie baby." Declaring our love in so many words. He really was inside my head. What is going on with me?

"Who said I wanted you to?" I teased.

"Allie, you are killing me," as he stepped to me once again. We were having this push-and-pull thing going on. I knew I had to get away, or I would be drawn magnetically into his bed.

I walked away, smiling from ear to ear as I approached my friends.

"What the fuck, Allie! You met him in Europe?!" Serena jumped into my arms, drooling from too much coke.

"Yes, yes...if you guys had given me five minutes to talk today, I would have told you. It's kind of complicated," yelling over the top of them.

"What's complicated...? Never mind, let's go to the Rose Bar lounge in the Gramercy Hotel. We can save this talk for tomorrow over our hangovers."

Packed with white powder dropping out of her nose, Serena dragged us out. Our hot mess of a friend was half the party. Who was I to tell her not to?

On the other hand, Beth was a boss momma. "Clean it up, you're a mess," wiping Serena's nose like a good friend.

"I don't know what I would do without you, mom," grabbing Beth and me, Serena pulled us relentlessly through the crowd toward the exit.

I was happy to be with my friends. Feeling this good was like a drug for me. I was somebody, not a wallflower. People looked at me; they looked at me like they do, Tory. The night was popping, and so was the Champagne. Rose Bar had been around for a while, but we still loved it. It had a substantial black bouncer that would never smile unless you gave him a 100-dollar bill. We didn't have to do that because we knew all of the owners and managers, but I still did because he had to put up with all of these people. We went to our favorite table in the center of the room. Serena wanted to dance and do coke, so she did. I got to catch up with Beth. Rose Bar was just that, rose red everywhere, the lush red velvet banquets, pattern carpet, and red lights, it felt like an old late 1800s Parisian spot. The kind of place I promised Dominique I would not be in.

It was a staple for us; we loved the place. Serena jumped from boy to boy there; she always had two or three dangling. She was so indecisive when it came to boys and love. Beth needed to know about the man at the loft party. "Raph... Let's see, I met him in St. Tropez at this place... a really cool place called Opera. I was on a date with Dominique. I went to the bathroom, and that's where I bumped into Raph. He came by and did Raph, flirted with me... teased a bit." Explaining to Beth the first night.

"Wait, wait, wait, Dominique, as in the man that was dating your fucking mom?" Beth's eyes were wild. She was onto me.

"Yes, that's the one," shrugging my shoulders with a half-smile. I knew that sounded wrong, but there was no way of explaining it in a busy lounge.

"What the fuck!" Screaming like she just saw a dead person, Beth was beside herself.

"Say nothing, ok!" I made her promise me.

"Yes, come on, you know me better than that, but I want to hear the rest." Grabbing my hands with concern, Beth was genuinely concerned. As I said, Beth was my protector. She needed to know I was ok, that no one hurt me. Serena rolled in behind us with drinks, "I probably won't remember, so it's safe with me." Of course, she wouldn't remember. We would relentlessly have to fill her in on our nights out. She had an issue with what we called a blackout. I never had one of those till I got much older; I'd have to say, it's not a funny experience. If you are smart, pass on the fifth drink.

I explained everything in detail for the next hour. My friends didn't interject once; they were glued to my every word. Serena could have caught flies; her mouth was wide open the entire time and let me tell you, this girl never shut up on coke. I ended my story with, "so that's it." "Holy shit, girl, that is so fucking hot!" Acknowledging my story, my friend Serena was actually proud.

"It's a good thing you have a French passport as well because the consent laws are fifteen there and seventeen here… You're right between the two." Beth spoke like an attorney when she had a valid point. I never thought about my age as a problem legally, but yes, this could be a massive one. I had to find out everything I should know and soon.

"I can help you look into it tomorrow. My dad will answer anything I ask. He's oblivious when it comes to girls. He still thinks I'm a virgin." Beth's father was a top attorney in New York City and had his own practice. Charles Hollingsworth was a Harvard guy, super dorky, super-intelligent, and yet so naïve when it came to his daughter.

We ended the evening and got our Uber uptown. "I love you guys," hugging my girlfriends, I was happy and depleted as I fell onto Beth's shoulder.

"We love you too. I'm happy you're back." Placing her hand to steady my weary head, Beth leaned down, kissing my forehead. The one girl I could always count on through thick and thin…to this day, she is still my sister in arms.

"I fucking love you ho's!" Serena slurred. She had a way with words. You couldn't help but love this train wreck. After all, she was our train wreck.

CHAPTER 22

Meeting or Meating?

The next morning Tory was up, which was a bit of a shock for me; usually, she was either out the door early or coming in early. Ida, our housekeeper, my nurturing friend, made us some breakfast; avocado mash and a poached egg. This was my favorite breakfast dish. Tory didn't know this, but Ida did.

"Good morning, sunshine," Ida called out; she was happy to see me.

"Good morning it is!" I also made time for her in the morning. After all, she was another person that got to see the good, bad and ugly, yet never judged any of it. Ida would continue to be with me well into my thirties.

"This is a breakfast meeting, not Ida and Allie bonding time." Calling out with her bitch boss voice, Tory was unpredictable now; I wasn't sure what I was getting from this moment on.

"So serious, Tory, try smiling." Poking her a bit, something I probably shouldn't do to her first thing in the morning.

"Allie, sit down. Don't push me today. I have a lot of shit going on. After all, I'm the only one paying for your luxurious lifestyle." Here we go, this bullshit again. She's relentless.

"Sorry," sipping on my tea, just waiting for the next command from the queen of mean.

"You need to go to Mr. Ruben's today, my attorney's office. He's good, actually, the best. If you need anything from me, call my assistant, ok. Allie, go handle your business! After all, you don't want me to interfere." Jumping to her feet, and waving her hand to dismiss me as she walked away from the table. Ok, that wasn't too bad; I could have sworn that would have gone down differently... "Whew, what a relief." You could hear my mother mumbling the f-word as the door closed. She was a piece of work. I was on cloud nine. Nothing could have made me sad today, nothing. I wasn't afraid of her any longer either, she knew it, and I felt empowered. Little did she know I also had to look at an apartment for Dominique and me.

I was getting dressed when I got a call from James John's camp.

"Hi, is this Allie Hart?" There was a female voice on the other end.

"Yes, this is her," I replied.

"Great! My name is Lina. I'm calling from James' New York division. We need you to come in today at 1 pm. You are going to be fitted for the private show we are conducting. Oh, and Allie... it's not a choice," explaining in her not-so-nice way.

"Ok, yes. I'll be there, not a problem," I agreed.

"Good answer, see you then." She rattled off the address.

Now I was reeling; this day couldn't get any better. Jumping up and down, screaming at the top of my lungs. Ida came running in, "Are you ok, Allie?" She asked in a panic.

"Yes, Ida, I'm better than ok!" She was a roly-poly Polish lady with gray ringlets. Little Ida stood around 5'2". She was there the day I moved into Manhattan. She was a grandmother to me; I loved her completely. I used to tell her that when I was older, with my own money, I would steal her away from Tory, she would come and take care of me, and I would take care of her. I think she believed my words because why else would she put up with my mother for so long? I did later in life bring her back to me.

I put on some red Rag & Bone skinny's and a black James skull t-shirt; I wore black and silver Golden Goose kicks and an ebony-faced silver Daytona Rolex. I didn't wear any makeup other than mascara and a little bronzer. My mother schooled me, so I kind of knew a little of what I might be walking into. I went to see the attorney first. I met Mr. Ruben; he went over the contract with light speed. Mr. Ruben had a second contract to cover all of my other modeling money as well. He basically said that Tory wanted me to only have 2,000 a month of my money until I turned eighteen, whereas I could have half, and then at twenty-one years old the remaining.

"I am ok with only receiving a certain amount of money, but I would like it to be more. Not to sound like a bitch Mr. Ruben, but I can't even shop on that," firmly crossing my arms. Seems I had a little Tory in me already. I didn't really want to shop, but I did, however, want to make sure I got as much as I could in my own private savings. I didn't trust Tory or her sharks.

"Allie, I will need to get your mother on the phone. Can you excuse me for a second?" Sweating as he shuffled out the door. He was just a drone to me, one of her many. I wondered what she would say. My thought was, she's going to flip out and call me. I sat in the office for around ten minutes alone before realizing he had left his notes. One of the papers read, as long as Tory Hart is the legal guardian of Allie Hart, she can keep the money in a trust. Wow, so that means if I could leave legally, she would not control my money. Now that's something to look at.

Mr. Ruben returned to the room a little shaken. He must have had one hell of a conversation with the tigress. "I spoke with your mother; after a not so easy conversation, she agreed to more money." Patting his forehead, grabbing for a glass of water, he waited for me to speak. "How much?" I asked. I am dying at this point; I wonder how much she settled on.

"Well, you know I had to reason with her. She did not want to budge. I have your best interest at heart, so I did my very best." Preaching on and on, this man doesn't have anyone's best interest at heart.

"Ok, I appreciate that," I responded with a small gesture of approval in hopes he would stop sweating all over the place. I think he was planting a seed to let me know he was working hard for me, an obvious ploy to keep me happy and not fire him when I became legal. He probably said the same to Tory. He was a slimy guy I didn't trust, not in the least.

"Your mother agreed to 4,000. I think it's a fair offer. She's being very generous," counseling me like a sworn enemy. He didn't know shit, but I held my tongue.

"That's better. I also want to be able to have 3,000 on my own credit card," I added.

"I think that can be arranged," he nodded.

"Great! I will just look these contracts over tonight, and I will bring them back tomorrow, sound ok with you?" Not really asking; I was leaving.

"Yes, that sounds good." His voice trailed behind me. I didn't turn to shake his hand because that would have been wet as well. I was physically nauseous leaving his office. I said my goodbyes with my contracts in tow. I was determined to see what the hell was in these lengthy documents, and I knew who would have my "true" best interest at heart.

Waving a yellow cab, I dialed Charles Hollingsworth.

"Hello, Allie, what can I do for you?" Mr. Hollingsworth, Beth's father, answered.

"Hi Mr. Hollingsworth, I'm sorry to bother you, but you said if I ever needed any advice, I could come to you." Beth's father was a good man. I knew he wouldn't let me down.

"First call me Charlie and second yes, I'm here...I meant it." Sincerely, I knew he did.

"I have contracts from my mother's attorney. I would like to know what they say before I sign them. I also want to know about a legal procedure called emancipation." I spoke a bit fast.

The word emancipation made me quite nervous. Tory would kill me if she thought I was leaving her. I ran out of time because we had pulled up to my next stop.

"Come by for dinner; we can talk beforehand. Ok, kiddo? I got you." Forming a plan with me was a relief. I could go into my next appointment feeling confident and at ease.

"Yes, perfect. I'll let Beth know. Thank you so much, Mr., I meant Charlie! See you later." I agreed to meet at 6 pm before dinner, paying for my car.

I enjoyed going to Beth's home. She had such an amazing family. They all loved one another, and joked about things when they sat down together. Charlie always told funny stories about when he was our age; his wife Helen would just smile and roll her eyes. Helen Haven Hollingsworth was a formidable woman herself. Helen was a psychiatrist and practiced with her friend Anna from school, Brown University. Helen looked like Beth but obviously older, and had a quick wit and a great smile. She was a happy lady in her life, her career, and most importantly, her husband, oh how she fawned over him. She taught me that it was ok, to love a man, to let him know. I always carried admiration for her. Helen would become an essential piece of my future.

CHAPTER 23

Hart Stopper, Show Maker

I was literally jumping out of my skin when I walked into the famous, 2 Gansevoort Lobby. Even the building James chose was over-the-top awesome. The building was located next to New York's famous Highline Park and the Whitney Museum. It was well known as an art experience open to the public; the art would rotate every six months. What it would be like to be an artist in this breathtaking space, I thought. I got my badge with my mugshot on it and headed to the James John offices. This was the beginning of my life as a working model. Things were about to get really interesting... soon.

James was the first thing I saw stepping off the elevator. I was shocked; he was here for my fitting? Men seem to have a massive habit of surprising me.

"Allie, come come." Immediately kissed my cheeks while pulling me to him.

"James, you're here. Wow, it's so great to see you again!" I was thrilled, James John here... now... this was the last thing I expected, really.

"Allie, you are my girl, my new face. I have to be here! This is my business, my empire." Energetically James spoke with passion. He couldn't wait to get started on all of it. He was always known for having a strong business head and always having a really good fucking time. His life was a party, but he was all in when it came down to company.

"I'm so thankful, James. This is every girl's dream...to work with such a cool brand. I mean, I'm in awe of your work." Gushing, I explained my love for the opportunity. He observed me closely, for what reason I am not sure at this point. Was I babbling like a fan? Did I have something in my teeth? He waited for a few minutes as we stood in silence. I didn't know what he was doing. I stayed quiet.

"Thank you, that is very kind." Wow, I was relieved he had something. I wasn't sure if this was a Mexican stand-off or something.

"Here's your contract.... signed," handing the papers to James who tossed them off to a young woman that magically appeared. We continued walking into the space.

I couldn't contain my huge grin; I was really here in James John's showroom. I felt like anything was possible. I was a strong girl now, no, a woman, in charge, fearless. I felt like I knew my mother better now because I was picking up some of her qualities; courage. I guess she wasn't all bad. Maybe she just had it bad in some of her life. My mother cracked a bit later in my early twenties, but not enough to really enjoy her. To this day, we aren't in a good place. I guess that is another story in itself.

"This is your team of experts - the one and only Mario Testino, your photographer; Matt is hair and make-up, Lou Lou is the one that will feed you, Aaron is on set today, and I'm going to dress you. I think that about covers it." Enthusiastically James waved his hands about. He was on fire today, with loads of good energy. You could see the designer was excited by my presence.

All the top experts in the field of beauty and fashion. They were all really kind to me. I assumed James told them I was new to this because they explained everything thoroughly. I did find it a bit odd that the designer would dress me, but what did I know? When I got to Mario Testino, I kind of froze. He was one of the world's top photographers. Mario had shot some of the most famous faces, from the Royal Family to Kate Moss, Naomi Campbell, and Madonna. The list could go on and on.

We got started on fitting me in some of his signature pieces. Crystal boots were paired with one of his rock band dresses; it was see-through and said KISS on it. Providing me with tiny cheeky underwear that barely covered my ass and, at James's request, no bra. There was only ever one man that saw me naked or even my breasts. Now I had a room full of cameras, a stylist, James John himself, and I was taking all of my clothes off, exposing myself. The funny part is I didn't mind it. I actually liked it.

The second outfit that was pulled for me was a pair of his pricey, money-beast high tops. These kicks had so many crystals, just dripping with blue, pink, and white. I was handed a pink crystal thong, a pair of baseball socks that said John, and a leather jacket. Now, this was not just a leather jacket. It was a piece of art itself. James called it the "Pink Paradise." Pink crystals adorned the jacket with femininity, and silver studs arranged neatly on the shoulders and collar made it ultra-edgy. Standing there again naked, I picked up the panties to hide my privates. As I pulled them up, I noticed James from the other side of the room, watching me, not moving his eyes for a second. Smiling at me, I got warm from it. I am not talking about my embarrassment. I am talking about my pussy. I didn't mean to bite my lip, but I found myself doing it and immediately stopped. He must have enjoyed it because he strolled over to me shortly after. "You look stunning in my clothes...you are made for me." With a boyish grin, James had no filters. He just went for it. I didn't know how to take that. Did he just say something in code? Was James hitting on me? Nah.

Thanking him shyly, he asked me to choose something from the racks that called out to me. Laughing, I said all of them. He wanted me to choose only one outfit, so I did. Just standing in his showroom, only two feet apart from him, yet I still hadn't put a top on. No one paid attention to our conversation; they were too busy getting everything set up for today's shoot. "Ok, let me see. If I had to pick one, it would be this." I glanced at his beautiful clothes. I chose a sexy, delicate little black dress with micro-rhinestones encrusted, a jewel buckle, and a plunging neckline.

"Fantastic choice Allie, very good. This is an amazing dress... It's yours, a gift." Handsome, hot, and now this. What else was in store with this mega-designer? I wanted to melt into his arms for a second, but I snapped to. He was one sexy, flirty man; I imagined my legs around his smiling face. I was really crushing on him. I had an incredible urge, and without thinking, that urge got the best of me.

"Thank you, thank you, that is so sweet of you," jumping into his arms, I embraced him. What the hell am I thinking? I am topless with a thong on and hugging the boss in this

208

showroom, in front of everyone.

"I'm sorry, I ... I ... I just got excited. I love the dress, thank you." Embarrassing myself was the very last thing I wanted to do. I was now warm in another place, my face.

"Listen, Allie, it's ok. At least I know you really like it," winking at me as if he were talking about something other than the dress.

I'm looking at him now, thinking to myself, how much could I be in love? I feel like I'm losing control of myself.

"This is surreal; you're an amazing designer, and you're a sweetheart as well." Gushing, I had gained a little confidence knowing that he could potentially like me. I wondered what his hands would be like on me. I felt like it was a great possibility. I didn't realize it at the time, but I was telling him that I wanted him. I was so young, I might as well have told him I was down with fucking.

"James, would you like to grab a drink while you are in town?" Slapping my mouth with my hand. Why did I say that? Why did I slap myself? He must think I'm crazy.

"I would really like that, Allie." Laughing at me as he yelled for his phone. A couple of months ago, I didn't know how to speak to a boy, let alone a man. Now James John is taking my cell number.

They put me in the Pink Paradise jacket, socks, and bling sneakers, directing me to Matt for hair and make-up. Matt was theatrical, charming, maybe all of twenty years old. You could guess that he was a proud, gay black man because he told me so. Matt was extremely feminine; he wore make-up himself.

"Ok lovely girl, I got you. We are going to make you a vixen, baby!" Pitching his voice like a soprano. Matt did exactly what he said he was going to. Doing my hair straight and sleek, parted down the middle. My eye makeup was dark and dramatic, even lining my already full lips. I felt like I was made up in honor of the Kardashians. It made me giggle to myself. Heading to set to meet Mario.

"Hi there, you look beautiful. Perfect for the clothes, James was right about you." Patting James on the back, acknowledging the designer's fantastic choice; me. James was in awe of me. I could see it because of his stare. It was really intense; he looked like a cat ready to pounce. Making me feel sexy and aroused, it was helping me get prepared for the camera. Did he do this for all of the models? I had hoped not.

"Thank you, Mario. I am so thrilled to be working with you. I've admired your work forever." Falling all over him like his biggest stalker. I embarrassed myself, but he didn't seem to mind. Mario was very kind and thorough. He put me in the center of the set that he had designed. Filled with silver, blue, white, and pink crystals in money signs. It was so "in your face" like my clothes. It screamed sex and power. Something I was beginning to embrace myself.

As we began shooting, everyone came on set, including James. He watched me intensely, enjoying my moves in front of the camera. I was a different girl now. I felt like I would burst from all of the sexual tension.

"Yes, whatever is happening, Allie, keep going with it. I love it," Mario cheered. I was so turned on having James look at me that way. I was making the moves for him. He knew it. We had this unspoken connection that wouldn't end here. The shoot was electrifying for everyone; they all commented on it. The day was so fucking long, but I was told repeatedly that I did great and that we got everything we needed. Changing quickly, I was tired, and all I could think about was an iced coffee and, of course, James, but I didn't see him.

"Allie, here's your dress Mr. John wanted you to have. He apologizes but has a meeting to run to, but he'll be in touch. Ok?" Lou Lou, his assistant, explained while handing me the garment bag. "Ok, thank you. Thank you for everything." I headed back uptown. I was beyond happy from the day, but a tiny part of me longed to walk out with him so that I could share alone time. Would he get in touch? Who knows anything?

CHAPTER 24

Get a Monkey off your Back

I made it back to my apartment but only had half an hour to take the dark make-up off and switch clothes. I had to be at Beth's at six o'clock to meet Charlie's father. I didn't like to be late. I left on time, so I felt pretty good on my drive over. My phone buzzed... surprise, I had a text message from James and one from Dominique. James read, "Come and join me for a drink later. I may not live if you don't." I responded to him right away without even thinking about Dominique. I wrote If I can save a life, then yes. '' I then went to Dominique's text, and it read, "I miss my angel, I am coming into New York sooner than expected. I think I can be in on Friday. How was the shoot? I love you, Allie." It's Monday already; that is just days away. How could I make a drink date with James? Am I crazy? There he was, professing his love, making plans to arrive earlier, and I'm conspiring with his friend. I felt confused and ashamed. I also felt scared to go and meet him for fear of what may go down between us. I, however, couldn't stop myself; I was too curious for my own good, and I had to meet him. I replied to my Dominique, "Hi love, the shoot was amazing. I can't type all of it here, but I will tell you all about it when you arrive. I love you, please let me know if you can make Friday. I am looking at the apartment tomorrow!" I was just about to put my phone in my bag, and it buzzed again, it was bad boy James John. He wrote, "such a nice girl, let's meet at 10 pm at my place. Lou Lou will send my driver for you." Fuck, he wants to meet at his place. I would be a lamb for the slaughter if I went there. Feeling a bit nervous, I wrote, "sounds good, can't wait."

I threw my phone in my bag, paid the driver, and headed up to my friend's apartment off Columbus Circle. They lived on the 40th floor of The Time Warner, which was directly on the park, and it was one of the most desirable locations. It was also home to unique shops, live music, and the world-famous Per Se restaurant. You couldn't get out of the restaurant without a bill in the thousands. I knew the doorman never had to stop, so I zipped into the elevator and made my way to my meeting with Charlie. I had ten minutes to spare and felt like everything was going my way. The doors opened; Beth stood in front of me.

"Get in here. We have until 6:15 now; my dad's still on the phone with the office." Dragging me into her room, I laughed; she needed to know how the shoot went.

"Well, how did it go today? Was James as stunning as you remembered?" Beth rattled on, asking a million questions before I could even answer.

"So awesome, I can't even begin to explain it. It was like a dream. Oh, and James, he asked me out!" Grinning from ear to ear, I told her about my hectic day with him and showed her some iPhone shots I had an assistant take.

"What, tell me when? Are you going to his place later?" Living on my every word, she could barely contain herself. She was so curious.

"I want to, but I also feel like I'm cheating on Dominique if I even go there and something happens," I explained my mixed feelings.

"I get it. I can't tell you what to do, Allie, but I would think you're playing with fire if you go. If Dominique finds out, it will hurt him. You would most likely not stay together. I think James would date you for a while. He's been with girls for one to three years and then gets tired. The way you described Dominique, he doesn't sound like he is going anywhere. I mean, he wants to buy a twenty-million-dollar apartment here!" Beth weighed in. She had some valid points, but I wasn't thinking of getting caught, and I also didn't want to break up with Dominique. I was just curious. I had to see it through.

"You are probably right, Beth, but I still want to go," whining loudly.

"Let's talk some more after dinner. Dad is ready to see you, okay?" Pulling me to my feet, she walked me down the hall to Charlie's office.

"Hello, come on in. Can you close the door behind you, Beth?" Charlie stood up to greet me, motioning for me to sit.

"Thank you for seeing me, Charlie." Pulling out the documents, and handing them over to him, it was another big part of my day, maybe more so than anything.

"This is a contract my money monster mother wants me to sign."

Charlie and Helen knew Tory very well; her business deals were big and splashy and messy. Sometimes she would have three lawsuits; she had sharks for attorneys, so she rarely lost. They also felt protective over me because they knew more than most about the physical and mental abuse I had endured.

"Let me have a look." Grabbing the heavy binder, Charlie skimmed through all the legal jargon for half an hour as I sat in silence. Charlie looked up at me, stood up, and cupped his hands. "First of all, your money needs to be free and clear to you on your eighteenth birthday. She has all sorts of shenanigans in this contract, and that causes the question: Will your money actually ever see your hands?" Charlie shook his head in disgust. Explaining that Tory had put in many stipulations about my mental health, inexperience, age, you name it, and she wrote it. Why she did all of this, that part is easy, she wanted control of my assets, and I haven't even earned them yet. Tory had no intention of handing anything over to me when I turned eighteen. My mother was trying to steal from me before making a dime.

"What can we do?" I was petrified. I really needed an ally, Charlie.

"Hire me as your attorney. I will make the contract work in your favor. I might have to state that you can have a third of your trust at eighteen. Then receive the other two-thirds when you turn twenty-one. I suggest you let me call Tory; she will be more receptive to listening. I will tell you this kiddo, she doesn't really have a choice; these days, the law protects minors making money and having careers. I'll tell you what, Allie, he sighed, the things you've endured I'm shocked you haven't emancipated yourself from her." Charlie divulged something I had already been reading up on; emancipation.

"Thank you so much, Charlie. You have no idea what this means to me. I feel so much better knowing you're on my side. Will you please be my attorney?" I sat on the edge of my seat, waiting for him to answer.

"Yes, Allie Hart, I will. Do you have a dollar?" Putting his hand out. I dug into my bag and could not find a dollar.

"I have a five." I held it up.

Grabbing the five from me, "thank you for the retainer!"

I had a plan and a well-known and respected lawyer; everything was going to be alright... Wasn't it?

The Hollingsworths had a large 4,000-square-foot apartment, very warm, and full of dark woods. The apartment had traditional furniture and a softness about it. Many picture frames filled the house, all of their travels together as a family. I loved coming here. It felt like a natural home. We dined on cherry-glazed lamb that Helen had baked. She would cook with Beth and me whenever she could pull herself away from work. Helen always made a point to make a family dinner once a week, nice and normal, I thought. Dinner was done, and it got late, so I couldn't finish up with Beth. I looked at my phone. I had a text from Lou Lou asking me for my address. I sent it over to her. I wasn't thinking; clearly, I was only thinking about myself. I wanted nothing more than to see him. I couldn't stop myself from being intrigued. So, what if he is a playboy? He wants to see me, no one else, just me. I said my goodbyes and left for the car.

CHAPTER 25

The Playboy and I

I couldn't help but be curious about his home. I had only read about the renovated six-bedroom, six-bathroom, two-and-a-half baths spread. It supposedly had five fireplaces and three outdoor spaces, including a garden, a south-facing terrace, and a landscaped roof deck, so the papers read. I pulled up to 71st Street, and his driver directed me where to go. A small man dressed in black welcomed me, explaining that Mr. John would be with me shortly. I was in amazement at all the crystal chandeliers and flowers. It had a lot of bling, just like his clothing; it was over the top, like him.

I was taken to a beautifully low-light living room with Champagne waiting on ice; a large tub of Russian caviar and blinis with crème fraiche placed just so. There were dozens of candles lit and beautiful vases of flowers everywhere. The room was lush, the sofas were light blue velvet, and the expensive tapestry pillows were everywhere. There were white marble tables and an opulent fireplace of gold-threaded marble. It was like something out of your wildest dreams. Was James planning on seducing me? I felt like he was. I was comfortable with Dominique, but how would I be with another man? James, to me, seemed like a hungry animal that lusted for sex. I stood in the room deciding where I wanted to sit, and in he walked... James.

"Welcome to my home," grinning with his sexy smile as he walked towards me. He'd startled me, so I jumped as I pushed my words out quickly.

"Thank you, I'm happy we could do this," extending my hand as if we had never met. Why am I acting like this? Relax, Allie, calm, you have this.

"Don't be nervous, I won't bite you... yet." Smiling like the devil, the sexy devil that he was.

"I'm not nervous, well maybe a little." My eyes met his. He had a penetrating look. I felt like it was burning directly in me as my body began to heat up. My nervous energy was shifting. What was going on? Did I want to cheat?

"Sit, please," directing me towards the large sofa, I sat down. James quickly sat next to me but gave me enough space to feel comfortable. "If I recall from my showroom in Monaco, you liked Champagne." Looking me over, he presented the bottle.

"I do. You remembered!" Bravely putting my hand on his knee but removing immediately. This man is a stranger to me, and he's friends with Dominique. He must not be that good of a friend, I thought. I had already told myself over and over nothing would happen. I was just going to stay for one drink; I was confident in that. James poured the Champagne while talking about the house. I was curious to know what he had done, so he explained it with passion. He was a hands-on person and was involved in every decision with the renovations of his super-sized townhouse.

Finishing our first glass reasonably quickly, he poured us both another. We talked about living in New York and what I like to do for fun. I was astonished at how nice this guy was. Smart, funny, charming, and obviously fucking hot.

"Please, try the caviar. I like this with the Champagne." Handing me a blini piled high with caviar. I wasn't hungry, but I ate it anyway. I didn't want to be rude. "So, may I ask you a personal question?" James changed his tone; he got more serious with what he was about to say.

"I'm almost afraid to say yes, but yes," I replied.

"Are you attracted to me?" I paused for a second. This was not what I expected. He doesn't waste any time, does he?

"I am, but I can't do this. I am dating Dominique. I can't hurt him." Explaining with heart, but did I even mean what I was saying; obviously, my mind was saying no. However, my body was giving a different answer.

"I know, but are you the only one in his life?" Questioning everything I had in just a few words. "I believe so. He told me I was." I was confused and wondered. Dominique is a handsome, wealthy global businessman. Why wouldn't he be with other women? He loves me and only me, or does he? Maybe James had a point; perhaps I was a naïve girl.

My head was spinning from Champagne and doubt.

"I'm sorry to have said that. Enough about him." James apologized as he took liberties, pulling himself closer to me. I wanted him closer. I could smell him, his sweet smell.

"I feel uncomfortable talking about it, so please let's not."

Demanding it to end, I felt strong and could put that thought somewhere else; the back of my mind. He was now next to me, looking, planning his next move. I'm clearly attracted to him; it was getting harder to deny.

"Allie, you are such a beautiful, smart woman. I am happy we met."

Placing his hand on my leg, I felt vibration all the way to my privates. Oh, my fucking god, he has his hand on me. I wanted only one thing, which was for him to slide it up between my legs. I was turning into a cat in heat. I was buzzed, not thinking clearly. He could take advantage of that.

"I'm going to kiss you," leaning in, gently putting his hand on the back of my neck and his lips softly on mine, I let him, I had to, I wanted this kiss so badly. His tongue was slowly moving in my mouth, as it got deeper and more passionate, I put my arms around his neck, and he knew he had me right where he wanted me. I was getting wet; I could feel it. I could see his raging hard-on through his jeans. Pulling me down onto the sofa, he laid on me. His body was on mine. I could feel his throbbing cock. I longed for it, but I wasn't sure if this was a mistake.

Pulling back from me, he smiled as he took off my shoes and pants. I didn't have any panties on, so I was all exposed for him. Unbuttoning my shirt, I didn't have a bra on either, so now he could see everything, absolutely everything.

"You're so sexy... nothing underneath, naughty, I like it. I can't tell you how turned on I was today when you hugged me. I had to leave because it was so hard to be around you. I need to lick your sweet little pussy."

Brushing my nipples with his tongue, he headed slowly down my body kissing everything on the way. Then there he was, between my legs, my legs that I gladly parted for him. I was dying for him to make me cum. I needed it, so I was blinded by my thirst for him to please me.

"I love the taste of you," devouring my pussy, he was made for it. This man was so fucking good at it. I knew that I could only hold on for a short time before letting myself cum on his face. Working away on my pussy like he knew it, he was so hungry for it. I couldn't hold it any longer. My cries were loud; I had to let go, "James, oh my god, James." I came so hard and long. James loved it, looking up at me with his devilish smile. It was his turn; he couldn't wait any longer; he looked like a wild beast, kicking off his shoes, unbuttoning his pants, ripping them off, all the while staring at me like a blood-thirsty vampire. Opening my eyes, I could see what he was doing, and I could not deny him what he wanted. All I could do now was submit to this virile man. He slid his big, hard cock in very slowly; he wanted to enjoy the entry into my tight pussy. James just knew that I didn't have a lot of men in my life. You could just tell. He pushed deep at the end, even deeper, as he began to move his hips fast into me. Wrapping my legs around him, returning my movements to mimic his. We both loved this, us, this feeling, he lost his mind over it.

"Baby, this feels so good; I've never felt this with anyone," moaning sounds of pleasure. I also loved it, loved his cock and his kiss, the flashiness of him. He was the opposite of Dominique. "I want you," he declared.

"You have me," I whispered. He thrust into me hard, pushing him to the edge he needed to release.

"Allie, I'm going to cum. I need to cum. Can I cum inside of you?" Pleading as he thrust deep into me for the last time. I said yes without hesitation. I wanted him to. "I'm cumming for you, Allie!" James was filling me with cum. I didn't even think of a condom. We were doing a photo shoot just hours ago, and now I'm laying with him on his sofa.

James was tender at the end. "You have bewitched me, young lady. Where have you been all of my life?" Nuzzling into my arm. It didn't feel fake. It felt like he really met it. I wasn't thinking about Dominique; that wouldn't come till later. I imagined a life with him; what would this be like? Could anyone really have him? I don't think so.

"Come with me," grabbing our clothes, he walked towards the elevator. Guiding me up to the top where the master bedroom was. It was pretty spectacular. A big white bed, luxurious and inviting, behind it was an entire wall of mirrors etched with gold. It was absolutely stunning. There was another white marble fireplace and a large chandelier with tons of cut glass hanging over the sitting area, of rich gold velvet sofas. This man had some rich taste, over the top, but I liked it a lot. He loved white and gold because the theme traveled into the master bath. James ran a shower, keeping the light very low everywhere. He put some lounge music on and lit the candles. "I want to clean you," teasing me excessively with his touch. I smiled at him, then took his face in my hands and gently kissed him. Reciprocating quickly, our passion began rebuilding. I really wanted more of him, and he did too.

"You haven't had enough?" He gloated.

"No, I want more," kissing him again, then another kiss and another. He worked my hands all over his body, directing me to his cock, rubbing it as he kissed me. I had him hard again. I was ready to do whatever he wanted. Pulling me out of the shower, dragging me wet and onto his bed. He laid me down gently, looking at me as he put his hard cock in deep. This time he wasn't going in slow; he thrust deep, fast, and hard for minutes, never once kissing me. He was ready to fill me up again; he wasn't holding back this time. This time it was more animalistic. It was all about him. I was surrendering, I loved how he felt, and I loved that it was a little rough.

"Fuck Allie." Screaming loudly as he came inside of me again. It didn't last long, but It was raw, all of it.

I will never forget his face, so determined, and his body so out of control, he needed me and my sex. I giggled a little. It was a delirious feeling after sex; it made me happy.

"Stay with me, stay for the night, hell stay forever, Allie," pulling his still semi-hard cock out of me while landing his face on my breasts. I turned to him, without thinking, I was too happy to think.

"I can stay for the night; I'm not too sure about forever yet," stroking his head. Shortly after, I decided I really did need a shower. I asked him to join me, but he said he had to check a message, so I proceeded to take one without him. I didn't know at the time, but James was up to something. That text he was making had something to do with me, but I wouldn't know about that for a long time. After showering, he pulled me close to him to spoon; it felt right for some reason as I drifted away.

The next morning was lovely; he brought me a small café macchiato to bed, waking me with his tantalizing smile. "Good morning, gorgeous. How did you sleep?" Handing me the coffee.

"Thank you, I slept great," I chirped. The coffee was delicious, and so was waking up to him. "Let's go to Sant Ambroeus for breakfast. I love this place," gently brushing my hair away from my eyes. My first thought was the press is going to be all over it. I can't do that. I still loved Dominique. I was overwhelmed with fear, fear of getting caught. However, part of me wanted to say yes; being seen with him was every girl's dream, including mine. I was with the "incredible" James John. My feelings were mixed, I didn't want to hurt anyone, so I had to say no.

"I think that's a bad idea. It would be all over the gossip news; you know that wouldn't be good timing. It would hurt Dominique, and I would look easy, sleeping with you after my first photo shoot." It was a no-brainer. He had to be joking, right? If it weren't for Dominique, I wouldn't even be here. How ironic I thought.

"Fuck that guy; he doesn't really deserve you. I know this for

224

a fact." Angrily he threw a pillow off the bed towards the bathroom. He clearly wasn't mad, but maybe he knew something. What was he holding back? What wasn't he telling me about Dominique? Why didn't he just use his ace in the hole?

"Do you know something that I don't?" Questioning him, as I feared the worse.

"I hear things Allie... everyone does in our group," hesitating, I could see he was still holding back.

"What, what is it?" I demanded.

"Ask him," cautioning me, not calling his friend out. I needed to know what he supposedly knew. Maybe he just wanted me for himself; putting doubt into my head would do the trick. Uncertainty and guilt were gaining more ground in my thoughts. I got dressed and walked to him in his closet.

"I really like you," looking down at my feet, I couldn't find any other word than I like you, so mortified.

"You look like a little girl when you say this. I really like you so much. I need to see you later, and you haven't even left." Admitting his feelings, he leaned in for a long kiss goodbye, "I'll call you later, ok." I smiled, leaving him at the front door. My short car ride was filled with questions; who's who in this game of love? I didn't know who to trust, not even myself. Tory was always a cheat, and now I am too. Maybe it's embedded in my DNA.

CHAPTER 26

Caught in the Act

I got home; no one was around, not even Ida. I did see a printout on the table of appointments for me. Of course, it was Tory's doing because it was with three of the top modeling agencies in NYC and in the world. Showering again, I moved to the closet to decide what to wear for the people who would scrutinize me today. I opted for a black House of Hart deconstructed t-shirt and a buckled accent pair of red Versace skinny jeans. I threw on my Balenciaga knit, high-top trainers and grabbed a small, silver Chanel fanny pack. I didn't think a lot of makeup was what they would want to see, so I put on a little tinted moisturizer and some bronzer. My eyebrows were thick, so they didn't need makeup. I added a bit of light dusty rose to my eyelids and applied a soft coat of mascara.

I was a little exhausted from the nighttime fun, but pulling it together, I was excited for another big day. Unplugging my phone, I took a look at my text messages. One of them was from Dominique. "I will be in on Saturday; sorry, I have meetings Friday that I can't cancel. I am missing you, angel, be safe. I love you." I could feel the blood drain from my face, feeling the shame of last night; ugh, I thought this was an enormous disaster. Regardless, I had to respond. "That's a shame. I miss you too, my love. Can't wait to see you Saturday." The other one was from Beth, "Call me, oh, and my dad said he was finished with your contract." Wow, that was fast, I thought. The contract is finished. It couldn't be better timing. I had signed half of a million-dollar deal with James and now this. Knowing I would have my own power, money, and freedom made me smile and soon forget about all of the boys. How could I get Tory out of my fucking hair for good? I needed a plan, but I couldn't rack my brain with the answer, but little did I know at the time the answer was already out in the universe. It would come back to me, and soon.

I got to the Ford Agency, walking in with confidence. I spoke to the receptionist, who happened to look like she could have modeled, bringing me to an office; she told me to sit down and make myself comfortable. A petite Asian woman came in shortly after and introduced herself as the CEO of Ford. Needless to say, I was a little thrown back.

"Hello Allie, I'm Nancy Chen; I'm the CEO of Ford," extending her hand out to shake mine.

"It's a pleasure to meet you, Nancy," smiling like I belonged. I gained confidence; it was attractive.

Explaining to me that she saw the James John photographs from my shoot. Nancy had got in touch with James at Tory's request, and he made sure she got a few sent digitally. Apparently, she and James also had a long and fruitful conversation about my future with his brand. Nancy was very positive, telling me that she saw the same star-quality that he did. I really liked her; she had a nice way of talking to me. I quickly knew I wanted to work with her. I was young, but I was beginning to suss people out reasonably quickly. I think it might have been something my mother inadvertently taught me. Later in life, that would serve me well, going with my gut feeling. I didn't want to see any other agencies until I could see her offer. So, I didn't

My phone rang, it was Tory, she would never call unless it was an emergency.

"I'm sorry, Nancy, this is my mother. It could be important," explaining while pulling my phone out. I would never in a lifetime answer my phone right now for anyone other than the queen herself. Nancy excused herself. I answered, "Tory, anything wrong?"

"Are you at Ford? If so, hurry it up. I'll pick you up with my driver in twenty minutes downstairs." Well, she wasn't drinking and didn't appear to be angry, so I felt relieved. Nancy returned, telling me her plans if I signed. I listened to every word; after all, this was the lady that I knew would represent me. Nancy made her points fairly quickly, giving me a physical copy of my contract to have my attorney check. While I decided if I wanted to sign. I was floating... and James had spoken on my behalf; this was shocking to me. Why is he helping me so much? Is it because he really does like me? Because of his reputation of falling in and out of love, I wondered if I would just end up getting crushed by a guy like that.

Tory was standing outside of her car talking on the phone. Jumping into the car, I waited for her to finish.

"Hello, Miss Allie." The driver, Bernie, turned around with a big smile. Bernie was probably about 60, bald, husky build, and stood around 6'4". He had been with us since I was twelve.

I met Bernie on my first day of school at Sacred Heart. He had witnessed me crying all the way in the car; I'll never forget how scared I was of the New York City girls. Those days are long gone, no crying Allie anymore.

"Hello Bernie, how are you today?" Patting him on the shoulder.

"I'm alive. What could be bad?" He joked. He was a happy man; I'll give him that. I don't know how he could be, riding with the "ice queen," but he was. Tory popped inside.

"I'll give you a ride home, and you can tell me how it went with Nancy Chen."

"Sure, Tory," I will tell her everything, but I refused to show her the contract.

"Don't keep me waiting, tell me about the meeting. Did she offer to sign you?" Demanding, I answer her and fast. I knew better, so I started talking. I told her that yes, she wanted to sign me and that we were to receive an offer the next day. Explaining that I wanted to work with her. That made my mother happy; she liked Nancy and the agency. Tory respected strong women in business, precisely what Nancy Chen was. My mother seemed genuinely interested. I felt like she had grown some newfound admiration for her little Allie.

"Ok, super. Let me have a look at the contracts," putting out her hand, but I pretended not to have them.

"I will send you the email after she sends it over," I replied.

I already had the hard copy, but there was zero chance I would be handing it over before I saw Charlie. I learned a lot from Tory, and I started putting it to good use.

"Ok, sounds good. George, I need a drink. St. Regis please," Tory ordered her driver.

This was one of her special spots. She loved her corner table, where the old waiter who had worked there forever treated her like royalty, and everyone in between kissed her ass.

"You're coming with me. I need some company." Tory didn't ask, she just told me.

"You want me to grab drinks with you?" I was shocked but happy.

"Do you see anyone else in the car?" Laughing a little to herself as she checked her phone.

I was pleasantly surprised, drinks with Tory. I didn't like her half of the time, but I did want her approval and love.

People noticed us, we were beautiful, and now I could pass for twenty-one. My mother, of course, had to say hello to a few people.

"Allie, grab me a Grey Goose Martini, dirty with one olive. I'll be right back; I have to make nice with a bunch of asshole men," smiling and waving as she walked towards them. Tory was a real piece of work, like a charming snake. I had a minute to check my messages, and a few were from my friends. They wanted to hang this evening, considering we had school in two days. The other one was from James; "I can't stop thinking about you. Where are you now?" I couldn't help but smile, he was a bad boy, and I liked being naughty. I was beginning to resemble someone else I knew, but I didn't realize it at the time. "Awe really? I'm with my mother at St. Regis; we are grabbing a drink." I wrote back. I didn't hear back from him after that.

My mother returned to the table with a handsome middle-aged man. He had an Italian accent with clothes to match.

"I brought a friend to join us," she smiled wickedly. I guess she found her prey; she didn't need me now, did she?

"Oh, did you now..? Hello, nice to meet you. Hey, wait, aren't you that actor... You were in a movie with Angelina Jolie, no?" Rambling on, I finally arrived at a question. Blue eyes, brown hair, I remember this fox from something.

"Yes, that's me. Shh, don't tell anyone else I'm hiding out at your table," he joked. They sat down, but before I could get his name, my phone rang, shit it was James.

"Can you excuse me, please?" As I left the bar, I entered the hall to grab the call. I wanted to hear his voice; he was dangerous in a good way. "Hello, you." I answered.

"What are you wearing?" Asking in a low, sexy voice.

"What?" I laughed.

"I asked, what are you wearing?" Repeating himself.

"Well, maybe I don't want to tell you." I teased.

"Turn around." His voice got louder. There he was James John, chasing me down at the St. Regis. I was flattered but also thought, what if people found out? This could stain my newfound career. I didn't listen to the little voice that said run. I listened to the big voice that screamed yes! I was also learning a little trick Tory told me about; compartmentalizing. The queen often schooled me about it and told me it was customary to love more than one person. I thought she had gone mad at the time, but now I'm thinking it sounds completely ok.

"I thought you wanted me to come. After all, you told me where you were," handing me a key card. He was standing there so nonchalant; he didn't care if a gang of paparazzi came running in. He was a man out for what he wanted, and I was it.

"What is this, James?" Questioning him, but I already knew the answer. It was a key to a room. "Milano Suite. Meet me there in five minutes, ok?" Begging, he put his hands together in a praying position, backing away slowly.

"You are terrible," nodding my head.

I should not be doing this, going upstairs with him while Tory was in the other room. My saving grace is the hot actor. Why shouldn't I go was the bigger question? "Meet you in five minutes." Walking back into the bar, I would make an excuse to leave.

"Tory, I need to get going. I have a thing with my friends." I said while taking a big gulp of the full glass of wine on the table.

"Ok, see you later. Have fun," waving me off as she continued with her conversation with the hot Italian.

"Nice to meet you," the man replied.

"Same never did catch your name," yelling back through the bar.

"It's Raoul." Okay, I thought Raoul, now I know, but how did she know him?

The St. Regis is of the utmost elegance, a five-star French Beaux-Arts style hotel, I had never seen the rooms, so I was curious to say the least. More importantly, I couldn't wait to see this man, I was beaming. I got to the door, entering with my key. Standing with a glass of Champagne and a naughty disposition was James.

"For you mademoiselle," handing me the glass.

"Thank you," I licked my lips. The lovely suite of soft pillows and soft tones filled the room. There was a large 18th-century mirror leaning against the wall next to the bed and another above it. I was impressed with the space, but I was more impressed that he came to see me. He had no fear; he was utterly rock and roll. I wanted him badly. I didn't care about the Champagne. I kept my composure for another sip.

I had only been in the room for three minutes, and I blurted it out, "I want you." I put my Champagne down, stepping to him so that I was only an inch from his lips. I didn't move. I waited. Grabbing my hand, and putting it on his cock.

"I want you too." It was stiff and throbbing. I could feel the blood pumping. He was like a lion ready to pounce. "Get over here." Clutching onto my shirt with both hands. I was hot for this man and prepared to feed him. We furiously grabbed, pulling one another's clothes off.

"Lay down and spread your beautiful legs for me." Demanding as he pushed me onto the king-size bed. I liked him manhandling me; he was just rough enough with me. I could barely wait seconds for him to enter me. Sliding his big hard cock into my wet pussy, we both laid out a sigh of ecstasy. It was a relief to be fed his beautiful manhood. I needed him like a person in a desert who needed water.

"Oh… Oh my god… You feel so good, James," I cried out, over and over, his name falling from my lips. I was filled up with the hot, sexy, wild beast. I would need more, much more.

"I love your pussy, so fucking tight and wet…. fuck I love this," howling, pushing harder, ordering me to touch my pussy. I played with myself while he thrust away. He pulled me up, flipping my body over to be on my hands and knees; he wanted to mount me like the animal he was. I wanted him to push harder; with him, it was different. I felt more alive, more adventurous. I craved his cock, even while he was fucking me.

"Play with yourself. I want you to cum with me, baby," fucking me deeply, as he ordered me to do what he wanted. I obliged, working my mound. I needed to cum with him. I knew somewhere in my head that this would bond us. Was I falling in love again, or was this pure lust? I never knew this could feel like this, so wild. I was into this bad boy, and I wasn't going to say no to him again.

"I'm close, my love; I'm going to cum now," I whimpered.

"Good girl, cum baby. I'm going to now; I'm going to fill up your tight little pussy. I'm fucking cumming, Allie," moaning deeply as he dug his hands into my ass. We came together. It was so vulgar and completely exhilarating. We were overtaken by this insane attraction to one another. I could feel his desire for me now more than ever. What lengths would he go to, to keep me all to himself? How could I stay away?

I wanted my cake and to eat it too. I still loved Dominique, that I felt, but I also wanted the attention that I was getting from James. We lay on the bed. I was still vibrating from the experience and reliving it in my head while I buried my smile in him. The funny thing is, it felt normal to be in his arms as well. Was he feeling that, too, or was he just interested in another notch in his belt? I don't know, but for now, I was enjoying myself.

"Allie, have dinner with me tonight. We can go anywhere you like," he pleaded. He knew that wasn't possible, but he kept trying.

"James, you know we can't," responding with a kiss.

"Well, I've always been known to throw a dinner party for the new face of James John, and that shouldn't stop now." He was very calculated to devise a plan for us to go out and not be seen as a couple. I was beginning to see it. He planned on throwing a huge dinner party downtown at an upscale restaurant that I loved called Le CouCou.

"Let me call Lou Lou and have her arrange a table for twenty." Dialing his phone, there was no stopping him, so I didn't.

"You are something. You never take no for an answer," rolling my eyes at this crazy, delicious man in front of me. Anyone that would add eighteen people so that he could have dinner with me had to be crazy. I got up, showered. I had to get back to my place and figure out what to wear. I had time, but I wanted to look amazing for this. After all, there would be loads of photographs taken.

"Ok, all settled. We have the table at nine o'clock, babe," grabbing my waist tightly. He was so strong and rough with me. I liked it; it was foreign to me.

"Thank you, that was a very sweet thing you did for me." Hugging his manful frame, I looked up, and he met me with a kiss.

"This is just the beginning, more to come," he promised. So fun. He made me laugh nonstop, he was so over the top, but he had a lot of success and wanted to share it. I thought to myself... I could see us together for a while, but would it last?

"I will see you soon, ok. I have to leave before you," kissing him quickly one last time before I ducked out of the hotel suite.

"I'll miss you." His voice trailed behind me as I walked to the elevator.

CHAPTER 27

James vs. Dominique

I got home and read something from my mother's attorney; I sent it over to Charlie. Tory saw blood in the water and was about to kill if I understood correctly. My phone rang a few minutes later, it was Charlie.

"Hey, kiddo, how are you?" He asked.

"I'm great Charlie, how are you today?" I was worried but glad he called right away.

"All the same here. Thanks for asking. Listen, kiddo, I read over the papers, and it does look like the same garbage as the first one. Don't sign anything." Charlie had my back, so I would do anything he said.

"There's something I wanted to ask you, Charlie, something I think could alleviate the problem." Telling him the plan I had devised; emancipation. Charlie was impressed, he thought that this might be our only option, and he was willing to give it go, his words, not mine. With Charlie managing my money and contracts, I'm sure he could get this done as well. I could taste freedom on the horizon, or could I? Maybe it was just hope; there was no way Tory would give up so quickly. I was in for a fight.

I hung up with him, turned on some music, and opened up a bottle of Chablis. I grew fond of French wine, actually all wine. Buzzing from the alcohol and delirious with happiness, I couldn't wait to see James's face again. I was longing for his attention. He was like a hunter, and I, the hunted, made it more exciting than anything. I had the new dress he had gifted me... short, shimmery, and perfect for tonight, but I needed a necklace to wear with the plunging neckline. I went to my mother's closet, pulling out a two-carat, green emerald necklace on a long gold chain. This will go perfectly with the ring Dominique got for me. I felt a little remorseful during all of the bliss, thinking about the love I professed to Dominique such a short time ago. What was I thinking, that he was perfect? I never had to worry about him cheating or leaving me. If he found out what I was up to, he would never forgive me. I had second thoughts about this thing I was having with James; I was acting silly with my little crush. I already leaped, and I knew it wouldn't be easy to end something with him. He doesn't take no for an answer; anyone could see that. Chugging down the wine, I proceeded to the kitchen to get another. I needed to ease my racing thoughts. Fuck this. I'll bring the whole bottle, I thought. This too, became the norm, drinking that is. You don't grow up in Manhattan, have a modeling contract, unlimited funds, and expect anything less; I was eventually going to lose my shit.

I assembled all my clothes on my bed neatly, almost like I was preparing for war; beauty war. Deciding to continue the brand's theme, I pulled out a pair of black John James skull heels; they were super sexy. James loved everything overly sexy. Styling my hair big and wavy, off to the side. I chose dramatic makeup; my smokey lids made my green eyes pop like a black panther. I felt extremely confident and ready for the big event. I would continue to do this ritual to this day. The love of preparing for a night out is almost as much fun as being there. James was right on time, waiting outside of my place exactly at 8:45, casually leaning against his Black Phantom. Wearing an all-black fitted suit with a John t-shirt under it. He looked fucking amazing; we resembled a famous couple you'd admire and stalk on the internet. Everyone would definitely want to be us; I think he knew this as well, so the hunt was on.

"You are absolutely the very most fucking delicious thing I have ever seen. Wow!" Looking me over like I was his last supper. James talked about how much he loved his dress on me, couldn't say enough about my eyes, and spoke of all of the ads I would be in. He even mentioned the cover of Vogue. He saw real potential, and he was cashing in on it first.

"You look very handsome, Mr. John," leaning in to kiss him ever so lightly on his smooth full lips, "You're killing me. I can't even have you kiss me." Pushing his hand onto his growing hard-on. I laughed it off, men and their hard-ons. We really did have the power, didn't we? As we were driving downtown, I wondered who was on the guest list. I didn't know yet, but there would be one person I never expected to see.

"I asked everyone to be there by 8:45 or not to even come. I want cameras on you and me. Especially the new face of James John." Sharing how we would enter, be announced, and that he only invited one member of the press that would also be there to cover the story.

"Well, I deeply appreciate everything you are doing for me," glancing at him with feeling behind my words. This man was motivated, but like all other men, he loved my innocence I still hadn't lost. At least not yet; that wouldn't happen for a while.

"You are welcome Allie, I know you... you are a good person." Leaning down, he kissed my hand, all the while looking up at me. He was as sweet as he was wild. Was I falling for him a little? Whatever I thought I was doing didn't matter. I should end this. I was playing with fire. I didn't know now, but that would never happen for a long time. He was a man that liked to win at anyone's cost. I would soon see this live and in person.

We pulled up to Le CouCou; a man was outside waiting for us. "Give me one minute to let them know you are here." Quickly the man rushed inside. He must have worked for James because everything was planned down to the second; James was good at planning "things" down to the second. Signaling us in, the man returned.

We didn't walk in like lovers, but he put my arm in his to be a gentleman. I let him; I didn't think it looked off. Entering through a set of large black velvet drapes led us to the well-appointed main room. The cameras were going off. James stayed for a few snaps. He had to be in the spotlight for a few seconds before stepping away from me, allowing me to steal the show.

"Isn't she perfect for James John?" Yelling proudly to the press and his friends. James's vice presidents and other essential people also attended; it was a scene. They were all there for me, the new face of the company. James introduced me to everyone. We answered a few questions and then sat down to begin the dinner party.

"You are my star. You did the Q & A perfectly! Are you sure you haven't done this before?" Laughing, James raised his glass and made a toast to me. I felt honored to be his muse. This was everything for me.

We didn't have to order anything because he ordered everything on the menu. Loads of Champagne kept coming, delicious wines; he even had everyone do a shot of 1942 Tequila at the end. We all agreed to party and headed to a club where James had several large tables reserved for us to dance. Even my girlfriends were coming to meet us. I couldn't wait for them to see me and for them to meet James, they were wildly in love with him through social media. I'm sure he would eat that right up. This would be a night to remember; well, that much is true. We were pretty lit up when the most unimaginable thing happened. I couldn't breathe for a few seconds as I choked down a sip of wine.

I had a clear view of the entryway from my chair that brought you into the restaurant. There was my love... Dominique! I saw him lean down and kiss another woman, the way he kissed me. He had love in his eyes. I couldn't believe what I was seeing. James was sitting next to me; I knew he could see this because he said something.

He leaned close to my ear, "this is what I wanted to tell you."

"Did you plan this James?" Questioning him while pools of water quickly filled my eyes.

"No, No, I promise you I would never deliberately hurt

you." He was adamant and stuck by his word. I didn't know what to do; they were heading toward us. Something inside me pulled it together, I stood up. I walked towards them, meeting them in the middle of the restaurant. Dominique was taken back; his mouth nearly hit the ground.

"So, you love me Dominique, with all of your heart, and you want to marry me? How could you? How?" I could barely get the words out as my voice quaked. The cries were too much to hold back now. The dam had broken, and so was my heart. My body was physically trembling as I turned to leave.

"Allie, please let me explain," grabbing my arm Dominique was desperate to explain. I could hear James now behind me.

"Dominique, take your fucking hand off her." Demanding him to do so, or he would remove it for him. Dominique did as he insisted but formed a plan verbally to walk me out and talk.

The girl he was with was sick of what she had witnessed and left the restaurant. I followed suit within seconds, so did Dominique and James. Outside, turning to both of them.

"James, thank you for being protective, but I need to speak to Dominique alone, ok?" I said to my protector.

"You're sure you're ok?" Concerned, he didn't want to leave me.

"I'll be fine, I promise," choking up an answer. He reluctantly went back in. I could not believe what was happening. I loved this man and thought he was perfect until three seconds ago. I cheated, but I didn't do it in public, and I was going to break it off, or so I planned. I was looking at an apartment for us, to move in together, hell ...I wanted to marry the man! Earlier I felt guilty for doing what I had done, but now all I could feel was my heartbreak. It literally felt like it was breaking inside.

"I loved you, wanted to move in with you, do anything for you. You said you loved me... You promised me you would never be with anyone else, you lied... you're a liar, Dominique!" Sobbing in the street, I was out of my head. I was shattered. I was completely and utterly devastated.

"I do love you, Allie. That was an old girlfriend; she didn't mean anything. I was trying to be nice to her. She just found out she is sick, very sick. I didn't mean, I, I, I should not have kissed her to make her happy. I wasn't going to sleep with her, I swear. I don't want anyone, Allie, but you. You are my angel." Dominique pulled me into his chest. I was so hurt and weak, I took solace and landed in his arms. I could smell his cologne and skin. I loved this man; I was dying now. I had to get away from him.

"I need time, ok. I just need time to process all of this. I can't look at you! You broke me... You broke my heart!" Pulling back from him in disbelief.

"Please, Allie! I meant everything I said to you. I don't know what I was thinking. I mean, it was not a passionate kiss; it was just a... fucking kiss. I promise you, baby, I will make it up to you... okay? Let me make it up to you, angel, let me make it up to you."

Holding my hands, he began to sob uncontrollably. Dominique was desperate. He needed to know that I wasn't going to disappear from him. Neither one of us knew what I was going to do.

I couldn't think clearly. Part of me wanted to believe everything he said; after all, I had an affair. I was in love. Truly in love with him, and to see that killed a part of me, of us.

"I need to be alone. I will talk to you tomorrow... I can't do this right now." Wiping my tears, I felt emptiness. This man I gave myself to ripped my heart out, all over one kiss.

"Can I drive you home?" Begging me over and over, he didn't want me walking in what I was wearing. This is what he was concerned about now? I felt angry for a second; how dare he try and control me. Then my anger turned to sadness, more sadness than I had ever felt in my entire lonely existence. Allie Hart, the joke, the fucking joke.

"No, I am going to walk for a while; I need to think. Please don't follow me. I mean it! Don't!" Walking away, I could hear him desperately calling out, "I will call you in the morning. We can work this out, Allie, we can!"

Confusion set in even more so when my thoughts turned to James. Was this a setup? Was he that calculated? I got angry, then felt hurt from what I thought he had just done to me. That I'm broken, and now he can have me, is that what he thinks he can do? This is my life; how could he play with people's lives like a puppet master? And my love, Dominique put his lips on hers like he did mine. No one forced him to do that; not even James could have planned for that. I texted James to let him know I was going home and that we could speak the next day. Even in a haze, I was smart enough not to ruin my career when it just began; he replied with a positive note telling me about the "already great photos that were taken and that he missed me." I guess it's good that we got the shot, right? He also got a shot at the prize, me. The question is, did he do all of this to break us up? If he did, what was I going to do with that?

I began sobbing again, and this time I couldn't contain it. Leaning my head back into a building, I wailed like a baby. I didn't care if anyone saw me. I just couldn't hold it in. I still remember the salt in my mouth from the tears flooding my face and lips. It could have happened yesterday... I can still taste it.

When my sobs subsided, I walked for a long while. I found myself in Tribeca. I was a zombie, I'm not quite sure how I made it to the building, but I did. Knocking on the door with my shoe, desperately waiting for it to open. Whimpering "Please open, please open." There he was, the face of an angel. One that could soothe my tears. He was the only person I could talk or be with right now. He alone was the only person I felt I could be safe with. I didn't even realize it until I got to his door. Raph opened his door, and I cried out, "Can I come in? I have nowhere else to go... I have nowhere else to go," blubbering my words until they were met with more tears. He looked at me with his beautiful, green eyes, the way he did the first day.

"What happened? Are you ok, Allie? You're not okay... come here, baby," pulling me gently into his arms. I was exhausted as I collapsed on him. Picking me up, he tenderly carried me inside, telling me everything was going to be alright. I knew I was in a safe place with him. I never questioned that; I just knew he was a good man. What would happen tomorrow or in the future wasn't important to me. I just knew I needed to feel safe. Raph was safe. He felt like home.

Acknowledgements

I know for some writing is a huge challenge, and believe me I have had my moments, but for the most part, the words in this story just poured out of me, mainly because some of the main character was me. I was locked up during the pandemic, like everyone on the planet, yet I thrived with my much-needed break from the everyday grind. I embraced the solitude and passionately wrote daily for up to twelve hours a day. I may have been forced to leave my home in France and now was locked up in a foreign space in Miami, but guess what, I was happy and I was in flow, so much that I wrote this book in twenty-one days. I had made friends with a core group of neighbors during my time in Miami in our little complex on the bay. With that said, thank you Roberto, Marta, and Court for opening your homes to me and making me laugh when I did break from my keyboard.

I would like to acknowledge the gratitude I have for my life partner Wim De Pundert, who always tells me to 'just go for it'. Not only did he believe in my writing abilities but supported me in many facets of my journey through the marketing aspects. Thank you for your continuous support and love, even more so your steadfast and unchanging faith in me and us even in the face of challenges, obstacles, and doubt. From the very moment I met you, Wim, I was completely inspired to do more and be more. I know we will always have obstacles in this life, but with you by my side, I could never be scared, because your strength is unwavering. Thank you, my cookie monster, I love you completely.

After writing my first two books, well let's just say, I did not enjoy the editing process quite as much, to say the least. I got introduced to Lucia Gillet, a fabulous writer and editor, by my friend Steven Lyon. He was working with this firefly on multiple projects. So, with that said, I will acknowledge the people that assisted in making it more than just a story. "Oh darling, love your fucking style," she would say in her high-pitched British accent. Lucia, thank you for editing my words to look a real novel. You work like a rockstar supernova. Steven Lyon, my friend and 'brother' of twenty years, you always believed in me, even when I had doubt in my capabilities. Also, you were wise enough to recommend Lucia, so thank you.

To one of my dearest friends, also an author, Caroline McBride, I have a list as long as my arm for my many thanks to you, my north star. You believe in me, you trust me, you honor the bond between us girls, and you have given me some of the most exceptional advice I have ever received from a single person; that includes my journey navigating the publishing world and my relationship I now have. As friends we have been through love and great loss. We've seen some of the most beautiful places on this planet together, but none of that compares to how beautiful your heart is.

Who would I be not to thank you, Rory, my mother. You had me when you were quite young, and for that alone, I believe it has to be the single most selfless acts a person can do for another, giving life when everyone in your life is opposed. You were a child having a child. You gave up so much to give me an opportunity to be successful in this world and always said I was special. Some may not understand you, but darling, I see you. I know you aren't the easiest of people to be around sometimes, but you are my mother, and that means a great deal to me. I love you for your flaws, I love you for helping my story flow with inspiration. I love you for your beauty, your badness, and your boldness. Thank you, Momma, I love you, always will.

To my sister, Jenny. You are like a daughter to me, someone I always wanted to protect. I want to thank you for being a friend and the little sister that defended me even if I was wrong. Thank you also for believing I was capable of anything when most people didn't even know my name. I love you, Arthur.

Thank you to my brother Brady for being so thankful daily that he has sisters. He always believed in me and always talked me up. "Hallie's so beautiful, Hallie's so smart" . . . You get the point. Thank you for always stroking my ego, Brady. I love you and your big smile.

I feel rewarded to have another sister come into my life at the end of the pandemic. I didn't know her my entire life but meeting her for the first time was remarkable. We spent an entire week alone and had endless conversations. It was natural, like we had known one another forever. Thank you to my sister Julie for looking at me like I matter; it makes me feel blessed and inspired to kick ass. I love you.

Many thanks for the support and love that I received throughout the years from some of the biggest hearts one girl could be so lucky to call her friends. Even when I was hard to be around, or when I was in some kind of debacle, you stuck by me.

Betsy, the earth angel. Cindi, my champion that could fly. La, the girl I had commonalities with. Johnny, my queen defender. Rupal, sleeping beauty. Daniela, my guru. Love you all.

I appreciate all of the help from the brilliant people at Softwood Self-Publishing. Nathan, so grateful to have chosen you to work with, although I am a firm believer that everything happens for a reason, including the choice of this bespoke company based out of the UK. Jasmine, for your professional and creative input, many thanks. Carl, the talented web designer that is making me look good. Maddy, happy to have found you on LinkedIn. Lorraine for your expertise and input. Thank you all for making it easier for people like me to navigate through the self-publishing world. You have made it an exciting adventure when it could have been anything but.

With my great surprise in this venture, I would like to extend a colossal thank you to Umut, a true visionary, for listening to my story with enthusiasm and for wanting to assist me in my plight to be heard in this world. Lars, thank you for seeing my passion for the project and always showing up to make it a reality.

Lastly, thank you Caitie for being my voice in my Unzipped sixteen audio book. I found you after listening to hundreds of others, but when I heard you speak at 1 am in the morning, I was jumping up and down like a kid.

You meet people in this life for all kinds of reasons. My reason is, I'm blessed.

I am humbled. Thank you all from the bottom of my heart.

About the Author

Hallie Hart is a prominent international artist, writer, and documentary film maker from New York City. She has exhibited her paintings in over twelve countries and is a part of the permanent collection in the prestigious Museo del Parco museum in Portofino, Italy. Hart opened her US Flag retrospect titled 'Unity' in her House of Hart gallery in Aspen during the pandemic to share a humanitarian message. Catching national news, 'Unity' became a public art event in May 2021, touring the United States, displaying her flags for all Americans.

Hart graduated from the University of Pennsylvania with a MA in English Literature. Her passion for creative writing spans decades, yet was never revealed until now. Hart currently finds herself deeply engaged in the canon of Erotic romance. In her debut novel *Unzipped Sixteen*, she brings the reader on a journey of an inexperienced young woman's path to discovering her own desires. A literary joyride filled with lust, love, opulence, celebrity, and fashion. Hart describes *Unzipped* as 'half-fiction' and says the books are based around her life.

Hart now resides between Belgium and the Côte d'Azur.